"You can't force me to go through with this, Liam. You can't force me into anything!"

"Physically, no," he agreed. "I'm counting on your sense of duty toward our son. He needs a stable environment. The kind money alone can't provide. For a start, think of what it would mean to him just to have you there when he gets home from school."

"You're still talking as if it's a foregone conclusion," Regan said jerkily.

"I'm still counting on that sense of duty," he returned. "Along with one or two other incentives."

She kept her voice steady by sheer effort of will. "Such as sex, for instance?"

Liam gave a faint smile. "It's a factor. A very vital factor."

KAY THORPE was born in Sheffield, England, in 1935. She tried out a variety of jobs after leaving school. Writing began as a hobby, becoming a way of life only after she had her first completed novel accepted for publication in 1968. Since then, she's written seventy books and lives now with her husband, son, German shepherd and lucky black cat on the outskirts of Chesterfield in Derbyshire. Her interests include reading, hiking and travel.

Kay Thorpe

BRIDE ON DEMAND

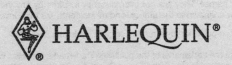

TORONTO • NEW YORK • LONDON
AMSTERDAM • PARIS • SYDNEY • HAMBURG
STOCKHOLM • ATHENS • TOKYO • MILAN • MADRID
PRAGUE • WARSAW • BUDAPEST • AUCKLAND

ISBN 0-373-12185-7

BRIDE ON DEMAND

First North American Publication 2001.

Copyright © 2000 by Kay Thorpe.

This edition published by arrangement with Harlequin Books S.A.

® and TM are trademarks of the publisher. Trademarks indicated with ® are registered in the United States Patent and Trademark Office, the Canadian Trade Marks Office and in other countries.

Visit us at www.eHarlequin.com

Printed in U.S.A.

CHAPTER ONE

GLIMPSED across a crowded room, the man was too far away for Regan to be wholly certain, but every instinct told her she was right. Liam Bentley! Of all the people in the world, he was the last she would have expected to see here—the last she would have wanted to see anywhere!

'Your glass is empty,' observed one of the men in the group she was with, in body if not in spirit, at the moment. 'Let me get you a refill.'

Regan released the glass with a smile and a word of thanks, finding it easier to accept the offer than decline on the grounds that she had had enough to drink. Alcohol was the lifeblood of these affairs, stimulating even the blasé to enjoyment of a kind. Not her kind, she had to admit. Any more than the majority of these people were her kind. It had been a mistake to come at all.

Where Hugh was at present she had no idea. He had asked her to accompany him because his wife was out of town; though for all she had seen of him since they had arrived, a partner hardly seemed necessary.

She caught another, clearer glimpse of the dark-haired man between shifting heads, and knew she hadn't been mistaken; those hard-hewn, handsome features were only too distinctive. Seven years hadn't dulled the memory, hard as she had tried to school herself to forget. More than ever she wished she hadn't come tonight.

'Gin and lime, wasn't it?' asked the man who had taken the glass from her, handing it over brimming once more. 'Cheers!' he added, lifting his own glass.

Regan repeated the toast but took only the barest sip, aware of the frank appraisal he was giving her. Dennis something or other, she believed his name was.

'Long hair is supposed to be passé this year, by all accounts,' he commented lightly, 'but it still appeals to most men.' He grinned. 'So does red hair and green eyes, if it comes to that.'

'Auburn, if you please,' Regan corrected with mock severity, making every effort to keep her party face going. 'And I never follow trends.'

'An individualist, eh? You've a lot in common with our hostess. She doesn't exactly run with the crowd either.'

'I haven't met her yet,' Regan admitted. 'Which is she?'

He turned to view the throng. 'Way over there, with that tall dark chap. Her latest. A banker, I believe. Loaded, naturally. Our Paula would hardly settle for anything less.'

The somewhat caustic note wasn't lost on Regan. A thwarted suitor himself, maybe? she wondered. The tall dark chap was Liam Bentley. Paula herself was a blonde; whether natural or assumed it was impossible to tell from this distance. Whichever, she was certainly good-looking. Not that Liam would be likely to settle for anything less either. Running her own highly successful PR company, the woman obviously had a good business head on her shoulders too. They should make the perfect pair—other partners disregarding.

Dennis had angled himself so that the two of them were cut off from the rest of the group. 'What say we go and find ourselves somewhere quieter to get to know one another?' he suggested now. 'There's still time to have dinner.'

'I'm not really hungry,' Regan prevaricated. 'The canapés they keep passing round are too tempting.'

'Just a drink, then?'

Obviously not one to take a hint, decided Regan resignedly. She shook her head. 'I don't think so, thanks. I'm quite happy here.'

'You don't look it,' he insisted. 'In fact you—'

'I'm with someone,' she broke in. 'I don't think he'd be any too thrilled if I walked off with another man. Anyway, it's time I started mingling a little more.'

'Whoever he is, he's not exactly attentive,' came the parting shot as she moved away.

Almost as if he had overheard the remark, Hugh appeared at her elbow, the unfairly rakish features wearing an apologetic expression.

'Sorry to leave you like that,' he said. 'I got tied up. Did you get to meet our hostess yet?'

'No,' Regan was bound to admit, adding hastily, 'It isn't really necessary.'

Hugh either didn't hear the protest or took no heed of it. Sliding an arm about her slender waist, he steered her round the intervening groups to where the woman was holding court.

'I thought it time we paid our respects, Paula,' he announced. 'This is Regan Holmes.'

The other woman's regard held a certain speculation though little warmth. 'Hallo.'

Regan returned the greeting, vibrantly aware of the man on Paula's far side. She forced herself to meet the steel-grey eyes square on as Paula performed introductions all round, uncertain whether relief or chagrin held the upper hand when he showed no sign of recognition, even of the name. He looked, she had to admit, very little different from when she had last seen him. Obviously more than could be said for her. But then, she'd only known him a few weeks. Hardly surprising if he failed to remember just one of his many past conquests. Best in the circumstances anyway.

Duty done, Paula turned an intimate little smile on him. 'Liam, darling, would you be an angel and freshen my glass for me?'

'Surely,' he agreed in those deep-timbred tones Regan recalled so well. 'You're in no urgent need at the moment?' he added, with obvious reference to her own barely touched glass.

She shook her head. 'I'm fine, thanks.'

Paula turned her attention back to the group at large as he moved off. Engrossed in animated discussion, neither Hugh nor anyone else appeared to notice when Regan slipped quietly away. What she needed was a breather— somewhere to be on her own for a few minutes. If it weren't for Hugh, she would cut out and head for home right now, but he wouldn't let her go alone and she hated to drag him away before he was ready.

She found her privacy in the bedroom where they had all deposited their outdoor wear. The early May evening was cool, and the bed was piled high. There would be a regular scrimmage if everyone decided to leave at the same time, she reflected. Like the rest of the house, the room itself was beautifully furnished and decorated. Money was no object to people in Paula Lambert's position.

Sitting down before the gracious Queen Anne dressing table, Regan took a cosmetic purse from her handbag and renewed her lipstick. There was no discernible shine on her small straight nose, but she dabbed at it anyway. Thick and glossy, her hair curved inwards below chin level to frame a face too full of character for conventional beauty, cheekbones prominent beneath wide-set eyes the colour of spring grass, mouth a trifle over-generous. Apart from the hairstyle, surely not *so* far from the way she had looked at twenty-two? she mused.

Liam would be thirty-seven now. An age when a man might be expected to start showing a little silver at the temples, a little thickening about the waistline. There might be a slight deepening of lines about eyes and mouth, perhaps, but the jawline was just as firm, the body just as fit beneath the well-cut lounge suit he was wearing. She could see in her mind's eye the bronzed breadth of his shoulders, the wiry curl of dark hair on his chest, the hard, ridged stomach muscle—and felt a warm trickle run down her spine at the memory.

Cut it out! she told herself harshly.

The opening of the door behind her jerked her abruptly out of her thoughts. Reflected in the mirror, Liam looked too overpoweringly familiar.

'So this is where you got to,' he said. 'I was beginning to think you must have left.' He paused, as if in anticipation of some comment from her, adding, when she stayed silent, 'It's been a long time.'

Regan gathered herself together to get to her feet, emotions concealed behind the social façade she had learned to don at will. 'I suppose it is.'

'There's no suppose about it.' He winged an ironic glance over the curves outlined by the sleekly fitting bodice of her dark green dress. 'Why make out not to know me just now?'

'I was following your lead,' she claimed with a dismissive little shrug.

The strong mouth slanted. 'I was under the impression I was following yours.'

'Seems we both misread the vibes, then.'

'Apparently.' He paused, the cynicism increasing as he studied her. 'The man you're with is married, I believe.'

The intimation was obvious, her response purely reflexive. 'So?'

'So can't you find a man of your own?'

She could scotch the impression right now by telling the simple truth, came the fleeting thought, but she didn't see why she should. 'I might ask our hostess the same question,' she said coolly. 'Always providing she knows your true status to start with, of course. How *is* your wife?'

'We were divorced several years ago.'

Thrown for a moment, Regan made an effort to control her inner emotions. 'I'm sorry.'

'Condolences unnecessary. We'd been living separate lives for some considerable time before it.'

'Oh, that does make a difference, of course. But then, your emotions never did run all that deep!' She drew a steadying breath. 'It's time we were both getting back to the party. Paula doesn't look the type to take too kindly to being abandoned for long.'

Liam swung the door fully closed again, standing there like a rock himself, face set in suddenly harsher lines. 'You know, I thought when I first laid eyes on you tonight how little you'd changed, but I was wrong. The girl I knew was nothing like you.'

The tone cut deep, drawing unstudied words to her lips. 'The girl you knew was a gullible fool just waiting to be taken advantage of! I learned to do the taking, that's all.'

The curl of his lip gave added weight to the wave of self-disgust, but it was too late for retraction. What the hell was it to do with him anyway? She drew herself up to her full five feet seven, still, even in heels, several vital inches short of matching his height. 'Are you going to let me pass? I don't think we have anything else to talk about.'

Something sparked momentarily in the grey eyes, then he shrugged and moved a step aside. 'After you.'

Regan hesitated, aware that to reach the door she would have to come within touching distance of him. Not that he was likely to touch her, she assured herself. He had already shown his contempt for what he believed she'd become. He could go on believing it too, for all she cared. His opinion was of no importance to her.

He made no move as she stalked past him. Her hand was on the doorknob when his arm snaked about her waist from behind, jerking her round to bring her up against him, his free hand coming up behind her head to hold her still as he brought his mouth down on hers.

Unable to free herself, Regan did her best to stay immobile in his grasp, but there was no denying the swift surging heat as her body awoke to sensations so long dormant. No other man had ever stirred her the way Liam had stirred her—the way he could stir her still. She moved against him instinctively, involuntarily, feeling his hardness, remembering the driving power in his loins.

She was shaky when he finally lifted his head, both mind and body in turmoil. She couldn't bring herself to meet his eyes.

'One department you haven't changed in,' he said sardonically. 'Save it for the boyfriend—if a man twenty years older than you are can be called that.'

Hurting inside, she thrust herself away from him and turned blindly to grope for the door handle. Paula was just emerging from the room opposite when she yanked the door open. The other woman looked from Regan to the man at her back with suddenly narrowed eyes.

'What's going on?' she demanded.

'A private matter,' said Liam flatly. 'Nothing for you to concern yourself over. I'm going to get a drink.'

He moved off down the corridor, tall, dark and unyielding, leaving the two of them standing there like dummies. Paula was first to recover. The icy probe she turned on Regan cut to the quick.

'I had an odd feeling that the two of you had met before,' she clipped. 'Just what game are you on?'

If the tone of the question hadn't alienated her, the instinctive dislike she had felt on first meeting the woman was strong enough to swamp any desire on Regan's part to offer explanation. For a brief disastrous moment the need to hit out at both her and Liam overruled all other concerns.

'Bringing up a child single-handed is no *game!*' she snapped back.

The other's face went rigid, eyes darkening. 'You're claiming to have had Liam's child!'

Realisation of what she had done hit Regan like a thunderbolt. What on earth had possessed her? she asked herself in consternation. More to the point, how did she retract?

'I'm going to get to the bottom of this!' Paula declared tautly before she could find the words. 'You wait right here!'

Regan forced frozen limbs into action as the other woman moved off in Liam's wake, mind devoid of everything but the need to get out of here. Turning back into the room she had so recently vacated, she tore her jacket from among the pile on the bed and slid it about her shoulders, then made for the door again. There were people in the hall when she got downstairs but no sign of either Paula or Liam, to her relief.

'Leaving already?' someone asked as she made her way through.

'Going on somewhere,' she answered quickly, and exited the house before any further questions could be put.

Only when she was outside in the cool night air did it occur to her that Hugh would wonder what on earth had happened to her, but it was too late now to start worrying about that. She set off alone along the echoing pavement, heading for the nearest tube station at Sloane Square. A bit risky for a woman on her own travelling on the underground at this hour, but she didn't have enough money on her for a taxi even if she could have found one.

No doubt Liam would have little difficulty in persuading Paula of the lack of truth in the allegation, but he was hardly going to be content to leave it at that, she thought hollowly. Hugh could provide him with her address. What she'd done to *his* reputation by not putting the record straight was no joke either. She was ninety-nine per cent sure that he was faithful to his wife. Hopefully, Liam was on his own in taking their relationship for anything but what it was.

She reached her small but cosy flat around eleven-thirty after an uneventful journey out to Kilburn, surprising Sarah, who hadn't been expecting her for at least another hour or so.

'Any time,' she said when Regan thanked her. 'With Don so tied up with this new job, I'm more often than not free of an evening, and it's hardly as though I've far to go home. Pop down for coffee in the morning if you feel like it,' she added at the door.

Coffee was the last thing on Regan's mind right now. Tomorrow was Saturday, which meant she would have to contact Hugh at his home in order to apologise for her unannounced departure—although what excuse she was going to come up with she couldn't think. For a wild moment she contemplated phoning him now on the mobile he carried everywhere and asking him not to tell anyone where she was to be found. A waste of time in any case, she realised, when all Liam had to do was look up her name in the phone book.

There was no movement from the bed when she opened the door. Regan went over and straightened out the tangle of small, pyjama-clad limbs and duvet without raising a murmur, bending to press a tender kiss to the tousled head. She loved the weekends when the two of them could spend quality time together—lived the whole week in anticipation of it. Nothing had changed in that respect. Nothing would. Liam was hardly likely to stake a claim.

Back in the living room, she opened up the sofa bed in preparation before beginning to undress. With only the one small bedroom, and allowing for the disparity in retirement times, it made sense for Jamie to have sole possession. She was lucky, she supposed, to have her own kitchen and bathroom for the rent she was paying—although that was likely to take a considerable hike when her lease came up for renewal next month. A bridge that would have to be crossed.

She was between sheets by midnight, though not to sleep. Lying on her back staring sightlessly at the ceiling, she went back over the events of the evening with almost masochistic intent. She could still feel the pressure of Liam's lips on hers, the hard muscularity of his body, dredging up memories she had fought so long to subdue. She hadn't been totally devoid of masculine company these past years, but there had been no one she had come close to forming any kind of relationship with. Her own feelings, or lack of them, aside, it took a special kind of man to retain an interest in a single mother.

Her heart gave a gigantic jerk as the intercom connected to the outer door of the building buzzed, settling to a painful throb. There was only one person who would be making a call at this hour: one person angry enough to disregard everything but the need for settlement.

The buzz came again, held for longer this time. If she didn't let him in there was a good chance that he'd rouse one of the other tenants. With Jamie fast asleep there was a possibility that she might still manage to keep his existence a secret, came the thought, as she rose reluctantly from the bed to switch on a lamp and go across to press the intercom button.

'Who is it?' she said warily, hoping against hope that it was a mistake after all.

'Who the hell do you think it is?' was the harsh retort. 'Open this door. Now!'

Short of risking others becoming involved, there was little choice. Regan clicked the control then returned to the bed, sliding her feet into a pair of slippers and pulling on a wrap. Catching a glimpse of her face in the nearby wall mirror, she lifted her chin, willing herself to stay calm and in control. That it was going to be an uncomfortable few minutes there was no doubt, but if she kept her head she could get through it without giving anything away.

She needed no second bidding to go and open the flat door in answer to the peremptory knock. Liam seemed to fill the doorway, the expression on his face a forecast of what was to come. He advanced without waiting for an invitation, forcing Regan to step aside in order to avoid being mown down.

'You've got some explaining to do,' he clipped.

She steeled herself afresh as she closed the door and

turned to view him. 'I apologise,' she said. 'It was a stupid thing to do.'

There was a certain sharpening in the penetrative quality of the grey eyes. 'Stupid isn't the word I'd use. Why? is the question I'd like answering.'

Her shrug was as indifferent as she could make it. 'Retaliation, of course.'

'A pretty unusual method of payback.'

She shrugged again. 'Pure spur of the moment. Anyway, I'm sure you'll have little difficulty convincing your…partner that there's no truth in it.'

'There's no partnership,' he said. 'Business *or* otherwise.'

Some nameless emotion flickered at the back of Regan's mind. 'Girlfriend, then. I'll write her a note admitting I lied, if you like.'

Liam regarded her narrowly for several seconds before shaking his head. 'Not necessary.' He cast a comprehensive glance about the room, opinion clearly expressed. 'Is this all there is?'

'I have a kitchen and bathroom.' She did her best not to sound defensive. 'What else is needed?'

'There's hardly room to swing a cat!'

'I don't have a cat.' Regan stirred restlessly, aware that every passing minute increased the danger. 'If you've said all you came to say, I'd like to get some sleep.'

The grey eyes returned to her, too perceptive by half. 'I haven't finished. Not by a long chalk. The man you were with tonight is a company director at Longmans.'

She lifted her chin, guessing what was coming. 'Right.'

'And you're his secretary—standing in for his wife who couldn't make it.'

'Right again.'

'So why the devil didn't you tell me that in the first place!'

'What difference would it have made?' she asked. 'Office affairs aren't exactly unheard of!'

He regarded her long and hard, ignoring the innuendo. '*Are* you having an affair with him?'

That's my affair, she hovered on the verge of retorting, biting it back on the reminder that it was Hugh's life she was messing with not just her own. 'No,' she admitted. 'I work for him, and occasionally socialise with him when Rosalyn is out of town—with her approval—but that's as far as it goes. He's a good friend, and I did him a thorough disservice.'

'No more than I did to the two of you.' Liam paused, expression difficult to decipher. 'I'd have expected you to be married with a family by now. That seemed to be your main ambition at twenty-two.'

Regan kept a steady tone with difficulty. 'I realised there was more to life.'

'And this is it?' he said with another disparaging glance around the room. 'You had it in you to do a whole lot better.'

'Compared with your lifestyle, I dare say this stinks,' she shot back, unable to maintain the composure, 'but it suits me!' Limbs shaky, she indicated the door. 'Just go, will you?'

'Longmans pay good rates,' he said as if she hadn't spoken. 'You must be earning enough to afford something a bit more up-market than a second-floor bedsitter— especially when you've only yourself to think about. I could put you on to a reliable agency if it's just a case of finding the right place.'

'I don't need any help! Not from you, or anyone!'

Regan was past caring about staying cool. Face flushed, eyes stormy, she yanked open the door. 'Get lost, Liam!'

'Now, that,' he remarked almost conversationally, 'is definitely more like the girl I once knew.'

'The naive little thing you pulled out of the ranks to entertain you for a few weeks?' Regan gave a brittle laugh. 'She wouldn't have said boo to a goose!'

'Not the way I remember it.' Liam's voice had softened, a smile touching his lips. 'The night I came back to the office to find you trying out my desk for size, you were far from being cowed.'

'On the premise that I might as well be hanged for a sheep as for a lamb,' she said, unable to stifle a reminiscent little smile of her own at the memory. 'I expected to be fired on the spot for daring to infiltrate the hallowed upper-floor premises!'

'Instead of which, you got yourself thoroughly kissed.'

Her smile vanished. 'And the rest! As I said before, I was naive as they come.'

'Irresistible,' Liam said softly. 'I'm not going to try apologising for the way I treated you. It's too late for that. It isn't too late to try making amends, though. I could help you get a job with better prospects for a start.'

Regan drew in a harsh breath. 'I'm perfectly happy with the one I have, thanks! Are you going to go, or do I have to call for help to throw you out?'

For all the impression the threat made on him, she might as well have saved her breath. 'I'll go when I'm good and ready,' he said. 'Right now I'd welcome a cup of coffee. Decaf, if you have it.'

Regan gazed at him in frustration, aware that she wasn't going to be calling on anyone to do anything at this hour of the morning. She knew a sudden sense of *déjà vu* as he shed his jacket and tossed it carelessly over a chair arm, muscle and sinew contracting as memory flooded in once more.

He'd always worn silk next to the skin. Her fingers itched to slide the length of his arms, feeling the muscular structure beneath the smoothness; to drift across the breadth of his shoulders and loosen his tie before beginning work on the buttons prohibiting contact with the warm male body beneath. She'd delighted in giving him pleasure—delighted in every aspect of their lovemaking.

She'd even believed him when he'd murmured words of love, she recalled cynically, bringing herself down to earth again with a thud. The shock when he'd told her he was getting married had been bad enough, the realisation that she was pregnant almost too much to bear. There had been a moment or two in the beginning, she had to admit, when she had contemplated abortion, but she could never have brought herself to go through with it.

'Coffee?' Liam repeated when she made no move. 'We still have a lot to talk about.'

Regan couldn't imagine what else there was to say, but it was obvious that he wasn't going to be shifted. Her biggest fear was that Jamie would waken at the sound of voices and get out of bed to investigate. At six, he was already protective of her, regarding any man who came to the flat with suspicion. Not that there had been any for some time now. Word got around.

She closed the door quietly, belting the cotton wrap more firmly about her waist as she made for the kitchen. The room was warm enough without turning on the gas fire because it gathered rising heat from the lower regions. Not that she gave a damn whether Liam found it comfortable or not.

He followed her, standing in the doorway while she put

the kettle on the boil and set a tray. The very feel of his
eyes on her back made her all fingers and thumbs.

'Why don't you go and sit down?' she exclaimed at
length. 'I'll bring it through when it's ready.'

'It's boiling now,' he pointed out. 'I'll carry it through
for you. Black for me, please.'

I know, she almost said, but that would have been too
much of a give-away. 'Sugar?' she asked with deliberation.

'None, thanks.'

He came all the way in to get the tray, his arm brushing
hers in the confined space. She caught a faint whiff of
aftershave—different from the one he had used when
they'd been together, but emotive all the same. The tremor
that ran the length of her spine left her weak at more than
the knees. It took everything she had to keep her face
from reflecting the turmoil going on inside her as she met
his gaze.

'Always the gentleman,' she mocked.

'If only on the surface,' he responded without rancour.
He ran his eyes over the tumbled auburn hair, softly lit
by the low-wattage overhead bulb, the captivating lines
of her face. 'You're still the only female I've ever known
who looks as good minus the make-up as with it.'

'Including your wife?' she asked silkily, then shook her
head in self-disgust. 'Forget I said that.'

'It's forgotten.' He indicated the door. 'Lead on.'

She did so, sinking into one of the two small armchairs
as he put the tray down on the low table set between them.
Without buttons to hold it closed, her wrap parted over
her knees. She drew the material across again swiftly, conscious of the brevity of the nightdress beneath and wishing she was wearing the satin pyjamas she had treated
herself to as a Christmas present from Jamie.

'You said we had a lot still to talk about,' she reminded him when he made no attempt to open conversation but simply sat there studying her. 'Such as what?'

'Such as where you disappeared to after you walked out of your job for a start. It was as if you'd vanished off the face of the earth!'

'I went home for a while,' she said flatly.

Dark brows drew together. 'You told me your parents were divorced, your father somewhere unknown, and your mother remarried to a man you had no time for and vice versa. That hardly sounds like home.'

'Nevertheless, it's where I went.' Regan ironed out any emotion from her voice. 'Why the follow-up, anyway?'

'Guilty conscience,' he admitted. 'I'd played you a lousy hand. I wanted to make sure you were okay.'

'Thoughtful of you.'

'Wasn't it?' The irony was self-directed. 'I know you've been with Longmans four years, but—'

'*How* do you know?' she demanded.

'I had a chat with your boss.'

Green eyes darkened. 'You'd no right to drag him into this!'

'I was under the impression he was already in it, if you remember.' He made a wry gesture. 'It's all right. I took full blame for the mistake.'

Whatever Hugh had told him about her, it obviously hadn't included the fact that she had a child, Regan reflected gratefully. All the same, she had to get Liam out of here.

'I really am tired,' she said, pretending to stifle a yawn against the back of her hand. 'I appreciate the offer to help me out, but it's totally unnecessary.' She added levelly, 'I hope I haven't caused you too much of a problem.'

His shrug was light. 'Nothing I can't handle. And the

offer still stands. You know where to contact me if you change your mind.'

He got to his feet, the coffee barely touched. Regan rose with him, picking up his jacket from the chair and holding it out for him to slide his arms into the sleeves. She was taken totally by surprise when he stepped closer to enclose her face between his cupped fingers, unable to form a protest as his lips found hers in a kiss that transported her right back to that first, never-to-be-forgotten time.

Senses swimming, she could summon neither the immediate will nor the strength to break free. The jacket dropped from hands turned nerveless, kicked aside by Liam as he drew her closer to bring her tingling breasts into contact with the hard breadth of his chest. His mouth was a source of infinite pleasure, soft and firm at one and the same time, persuading her lips to part, to allow him access to the tender flesh within, the silky caress of his tongue arousing an unbridled response.

'I want you,' he breathed. 'I always wanted you!'

So much so that he married someone else, came the thought, dragging her back from the brink.

'Just go, will you?' she said huskily. 'I'm not playing that game again!'

Anticipating dissension, and ready for it, she was taken aback when he released her with a wry little shrug.

'If that's what you really want.'

'It is.' She made every effort to infuse certainty into her voice. 'And I'm sorry for the trouble I've caused between you and Paula.'

His smile was fleeting. 'No, you're not. As a matter of fact, you've done me a favour.'

'Oh, sure! You were racking your brains for an excuse to dump her!' Limbs shaky, Regan bent to pick up his jacket from the floor, holding it out to him, eyes dark green pools. 'Since when did you need help in that direction?'

He took the jacket from her and put it on without responding to the accusation, expression unrevealing. 'It was good seeing you again, regardless,' he said. 'Take care.'

He was gone before she could draw breath to answer, leaving her standing there like a dummy. She had to force herself into movement, going over to lock the door in his wake. She still had her secret; that was all that mattered. It *had* to be all that mattered!

CHAPTER TWO

HUGH proved more intrigued than angry about the mix-up.

'I gather Bentley has something of a proprietary interest in you himself,' he said on Monday morning when Regan apologised to him. 'A pretty long-standing one in fact. Paula was spitting cobs when he walked out on her. Not that I can blame him. She didn't exactly keep the discussion under wraps.' He paused, eyeing her shrewdly. 'He *is* the father, isn't he?'

There was little point in attempting to deny it, Regan acknowledged. 'Yes,' she said. 'And thanks for not telling him about Jamie.'

'I was in a bit of a dilemma, considering you'd already apparently let the cat out of the bag, but I reckoned you'd sort it out for yourself. What I can't understand,' he added curiously, 'is why you kept it from him to start with. You were entitled to maintenance at the very least.'

'I didn't want *anything* from him!' she said with force. 'I still don't. Jamie's mine!'

'Does he feel the same way now he knows about him?' Hugh raised his eyebrows when she failed to respond. 'You still haven't told him?'

'No.' Regan looked down pointedly at the notebook ready-opened on her knee, wishing, not for the first time, that he would use a dictating machine like most people did these days. 'You were giving me a letter.'

The hint was ignored, curiosity still unsatisfied. 'Assuming he followed you home, as he said he was going to do, how the devil did you manage to keep him from finding out?'

'Jamie was in bed. I convinced him I'd simply been indulging in a little payback.' She put pencil to paper. 'All's well that ends well.'

Payback for what, exactly? was the question obviously hovering on Hugh's lips, but he refrained from voicing it, for which she was thankful. Suggesting he mind his own business was hardly on the cards when she'd involved him in the situation herself. Hopefully, he would let the subject drop.

He did. For the time being, at any rate. Whether he would be content to let it go completely was something else. The problem with becoming personal friends with one's boss, Regan reflected a trifle wryly. He'd have already put Rosalyn in the picture for sure.

Try as she might, she hadn't been able to put Liam out of mind herself over the weekend. Seeing him again, having him near her again, had eroded every bit of armour she had built up over the years. She'd wanted him the same way he'd wanted her Friday night—hadn't been able to sleep for the hunger he had aroused in her. It had been so long since she'd felt that need; so long since her whole body had come alive that way.

And it had to stop right here! she told herself forcibly, concentrating on the VDU in front of her. Cliché or no cliché, the past was a closed book from now on.

Except that it wasn't, because Liam wouldn't allow it to be. He was waiting when she left the office at five, standing by a gunmetal-grey Jaguar parked on double yellow lines.

'I'm due a ticket,' he said, nodding in the direction of a purposefully approaching traffic warden. 'If you get in without argument we can be away before she gets here. We need to talk.'

Regan vacillated momentarily before giving in to the undeniably stronger urge and sliding into the front passenger seat. Liam closed the door and went round to get behind the wheel, firing the ignition with a flick of a lean brown wrist and heading out into the traffic stream with scant regard for the outraged hoots of those forced to give way.

'Needs must when the devil drives,' he remarked, looking anything but penitent. 'That's a very disappointed lady we've left back there.'

'It's a very reluctant lady you have in here,' Regan returned coolly, mustering her reserves. 'If it hadn't been for the warden—'

'I know. You'd have given me my marching orders. Not that I'd have accepted them. You were coming with me whether you liked it or not.'

She gave him a swift glance, taking in the set of his jaw, the glint in his eyes—feeling her stomach muscles start to curl again. 'Is that a fact?' was all she could come up with.

'Sure is.' His lips stretched in a brief smile. 'Like I said, we need to talk.'

'We said all there was to say the other night,' she retorted.

'Not nearly! We've seven years to fill in for starters.'

Regan kept her tone level with an effort. 'I've no intention of rehashing the past. I'd be grateful if you'd drop me off along here. I've a train to catch.'

'What's the hurry?' he asked. 'You've no one waiting for you to get home.'

Her heart jerked. 'That's hardly the point.'

'I think it is. I don't have anyone waiting for me either,

so why don't we go and find somewhere quiet and peaceful where we can relax over a drink? Soft only, in my case,' he added as she made to speak. 'I never touch alcohol when I'm driving.'

'Very responsible of you,' she commented with a caustic edge she couldn't quite eradicate. 'A model citizen at last!'

It was Liam's turn to slant a glance, eyes narrowed a little. 'I wouldn't go as far as that, but we all learn as we go along. You've changed a great deal yourself. In some ways, at any rate.'

'I've changed, period,' she said flatly. 'I'll be thirty in a couple of months. That makes me a mature woman.'

'Age has damn all to do with it!' he scoffed. 'It's in the mind not the body. If you consider yourself mature, you'll stop playing the reluctant maiden and join me in that drink.'

Short of leaping from the car, did she have a choice? Regan asked herself. Sarah was used to her being late home after battling through the rush hour, and would have given Jamie his tea as usual. Providing she got there in time to have half an hour or so with him before he went to bed, he would be fine.

Only this had to be it so far as Liam was concerned. One drink, then goodbye.

He took her to a backstreet inn she wouldn't have known existed, driving into the rear yard with the authority of entitlement.

'My watering hole for many a long year,' he said in reply to her unspoken question. 'The landlord granted me parking rights on the strength of it. They serve pretty good bar meals if you're feeling hungry.'

'Just a drink,' Regan reiterated, already beginning to regret having agreed to even that much. He would have accepted the refusal if she'd made it firm enough: he would have had to accept it.

Broad shoulders lifted in tolerant acknowledgment. 'Whatever you say.'

There were only three other people in the small, unspoiled Victorian-period bar at present. Liam seated her in one of the cushioned, high-backed alcoves before going to rap on the polished mahogany counter in order to attract attention from whoever was supposed to be serving.

The big bluff man who appeared offered a casual greeting. Regan could hear the sound of voices, underlaid by music, coming from some unseen source.

'The taproom's through the other side,' Liam explained when he brought their drinks over. 'It gets pretty busy in there. Hardly hear yourselves think, much less talk.'

He seated himself opposite, still too close for comfort with only the wrought-iron table between them, his foot touching one of hers. Regan controlled the impulse to draw sharply away, settling for a slower movement instead. Even so, she could tell from the glimmer of amusement in the grey eyes that he was only too well aware of her response to the contact.

'Nice place,' she said in an effort to sound natural. 'There can't be all that many left unmodernised.'

'One of the blights of today's cultural trends,' Liam agreed. 'Which dispenses with the small talk. We have more vital subjects to discuss.'

Green eyes held grey for several, heart-thudding moments. 'Such as what?' Regan managed with creditable calm.

'Such as where we go from here, having found one another again.'

The thudding increased to a sudden crescendo, diminishing again as she reviewed the situation. 'You mean

now?' she asked with deliberation. 'A quick visit to your
flat, perhaps, for old times' sake?'

'Stop playing the cynic,' he retorted. 'That wasn't what
I meant, and you know it. Not,' he tagged on with a glint,
'that it would have been such a *quick* visit.'

Regan could imagine. His lovemaking had never been
a hurried affair. Her inner thighs went into sudden spasm
at the very thought. It was all she could do to conceal the
emotions coursing through her.

'Self-confidence you never lacked,' she said acidly.
'There was a time when it might have impressed me, but
not any more.'

'You prefer wimps these days?' he queried. 'Men you
can manipulate?'

'There's such a thing as moderation,' she flashed. 'Not
that you're likely to understand what I'm talking about.
It was always *your* needs that came first with you!' She
flushed as one dark brow rose in ironical comment. 'Out
of bed, at any rate.'

'Thanks for the qualification,' he said. 'I'd hate to be
labelled a selfish lover.'

'Oh, I doubt if you ever give less than full satisfaction
in *that* department!' This time she was unable to keep the
bitterness entirely at bay. She took a swallow of the gin
and tonic he had ordered for her, coughing as the spirit
caught the back of her throat, her eyes watering.

'Try taking it a little more slowly,' advised Liam with
dry inflection. 'Or not at all, if you're only using it as a
prop. I didn't bring you here to trade insults,' he went on
when she made no answer. 'I've a genuine interest.' He
studied her across the table, taking in the fine boning of
her face, the heavily fringed green eyes and full, mobile
mouth, his expression causing her heart to start hammer-
ing again. 'Who wouldn't have?' he added softly.

Get out now! urged a small voice in her inner ear, but her limbs refused to obey instructions to move. She gazed back at him wordlessly, devouring the lean masculine features, the thick dark hair her fingers itched, as of old, to tangle with. He was, and always had been, a man most women would find enthralling by very virtue of the fact that he was so utterly male in a world where the demarcation lines were no longer as manifest as once they'd been. Such a thing as moderation, she had said a moment or two ago, but it didn't mean a great deal at this precise moment.

'Are you still in the same flat?' she heard herself asking.

He shook his head. 'I've moved on a piece since then.'

'But you're still with Chantry's?'

'That's right.'

'Well up the tree by now, I imagine.'

'Some way to go yet.' His lips slanted. 'We're back to the small talk.'

'No, we're not,' she countered. 'As you said, we've seven years to fill in.'

'Not all from my side, though. Apart from you working for Longmans, and living in conditions that could be bettered, I know nothing about your life.'

He wasn't going to know either, she thought, stirring herself to action with an ostentatious glance at her watch. 'There's nothing really worth telling. In any case, it's time I got on my way.'

'You'll be right in the thick of it if you leave now,' Liam pointed out. 'Let things quieten down a bit, then I'll drive you home.'

'No!' The refusal came out too tersely, drawing a sudden line between the dark brows; Regan made haste to amend the impression. 'It's too far out of your way.'

'How would you know that when you don't know where I live these days?' he asked reasonably. 'Anyway, I don't have anything else on the agenda.'

'Not for want of opportunity, I'm sure.'

The sarcasm drew a shrug. 'Depends on the kind of opportunity we're talking about. I take life rather more gently these days. Which brings us back to where we left off,' he added before she could make any further comment. 'You don't mean to tell me nothing of any note at all occurred in seven years!'

Regan kept her tone carefully bland. 'I've had my moments.'

'And that's as far as you're prepared to go.' The dark head inclined. 'Far be it from me to pressure you. Why don't we eat while we're waiting? Save bothering later on.'

The temptation to extend the occasion was there, she had to admit. She rallied her forces to resist it. 'I already told you I'm not hungry, but don't let me stop you. I can still take the train.'

'And I already told you I'd drive you home.' Liam sounded just a mite intolerant. 'Relax, will you? There's no ulterior motive.'

'It didn't occur to me that there was,' she denied.

'Yes, it did. You think I might try something on. Well, rest easy on that score. I haven't reached the desperation stage as yet.' He searched her face again, eyes penetrating her defences. 'About you, I'm not so sure. You look decidedly unfulfilled.'

'As a psychologist, you make a good milkman,' she responded cuttingly. 'I don't need a man to fulfil me!'

'So you admit there isn't one in your life at present?'

'I admit nothing.' Regan was fast becoming unravelled.

'You can probe till you're blue in the face for all the good it will do you! My private life is…private!'

'Temper,' he chided, the glint in his eyes not wholly of amusement. 'You're losing your grip.'

She quelled the retort rising to her lips, aware of other eyes on the pair of them. 'A momentary lapse. The traffic isn't going to ease up for another couple of hours so I'll pass on the lift. There are times when it's quicker by train.'

'Except that there's no terminal within easy walking distance of this place.' Liam wasn't giving an inch. 'If you really must leave now, I'll take you regardless of the traffic. At least you'll be sitting down in comfort, not strap-hanging.'

She had to grant him that much. Getting a seat on a train at this time of day was a rare thing indeed. Only last week she'd found herself crushed next to a man who had taken advantage of their closeness to start running a hand along her leg—until she had changed his mind with a well-aimed heel in the unprotected top of his foot. He'd limped off the train at the next station with, hopefully, a lesson learned. But he hadn't been the first, and no doubt wouldn't be the last to indulge his base impulses.

'Regan?' Liam was eying her quizzically.

'All right,' she said, resigning herself to the inevitable. 'Just don't expect to be invited in on the strength of it.'

'No strings attached,' he assured her. 'Don't bother finishing the drink. You didn't really want it in the first place.'

Regan didn't attempt to deny it. She was here because there was a part of her that still found it impossible to regard him with the contempt he merited for past maltreatment—a part of her that yearned to give way to the emotions he still aroused in her. If it hadn't been for

Jamie, she might even have been tempted to go along with what he was suggesting and renew the affair.

Laying herself open to further hurt when he'd exhausted what new potential he fancied she might offer, came the cynical thought. It was academic anyway.

Liam revealed a remarkable knowledge of the inner-city road system and managed to avoid the worst of the congestion. All the same, it was almost a quarter to seven by the time they reached their destination.

'So this is it?' he said when Regan made to get out of the car with a murmured word of thanks. 'I don't get to see you again?'

'There isn't any point,' she responded levelly.

His shrug was more sensed than seen. 'A matter of opinion, but have it your own way.'

He drew away the moment she was out of the car, leaving her standing on the pavement feeling dull and depressed at the thought of never seeing him again. Yet what alternative was there? If she'd told him about Jamie he'd ten to one have felt bound to make some kind of financial reparation, but that would have been as far as it went. She was better off putting the whole affair to the back of her mind again.

Which was easier said than done. Jamie himself was drawn to comment on her absentmindedness when he was in the bath and she handed him the back-brush instead of the toy submarine he had requested.

'You're thinking about something else, aren't you?' he said.

'Work,' Regan improvised. 'It's been a busy day.'

'Is that why you were late coming home?'

It wasn't in her nature to lie, but this was one time when it was expedient. 'Yes. Am I going to drive the battleship tonight?'

'Ships are sailed,' he corrected in the tolerant tone adopted by most males towards unmechanically-minded females.

'Sail, then.' Regan kept a straight face, resisting the urge to hug the small, sturdy body. With his mop of reddish hair and green eyes, he resembled her rather than his father, but there was a certain something emerging in his facial bone structure, even now, that struck a bell—especially after having seen the man in question so recently. Not that there was any doubt as to his parentage, anyway. Liam had been her first, and only, lover.

She did a few odd tasks after he was in bed, watched television for an hour or so, then attempted to pass some time reading, though her mind wasn't on the written word. When the telephone rang at half past ten she was on the verge of retiring for the night. Liam's voice sounded so close, so intimate.

'I can't stop thinking about you,' he said softly. 'I want you here with me right now, your hair spread across the pillow, your mouth yearning for my kisses, your body vibrating with desire for my touch! You were always so giving—so utterly without artifice!'

'The word you're looking for is artless,' she said in an attempt to stem the swift-rising heat.

His laugh came low. 'I know what I'm looking for. The girl I knew seven years ago is still there somewhere, lurking under that veneer. I aim to find her again.'

'You'd have a long search.' Regan was amazed at her surface composure, considering the furore going on inside her. 'It's no veneer, Liam. I'm a different person.'

The one you made me, she might have added.

'We'll see,' he said. 'Goodnight, green eyes.'

He'd called her that in the past as a term of endearment. Replacing the receiver, Regan did her best to calm her inner tumult. It meant nothing. All he was in need of right now was a warm, responsive female body to share his bed; hers just happened to be the first name to spring to mind.

She tremored as memory ran riot, forming tangible images in her mind's eye: that lean hard body stripped of all clothing and fully aroused, the ripple of muscle beneath her fingers, the electric prickle of his chest hair against her nipples. In Liam's arms she had known no reticence, no inhibition. He had taught her so much about her own bodily needs.

There had been times during these past years when she had yearned to know that fulfilment again, but she'd still to meet someone who could make her feel even a fraction of what she'd felt for Liam.

What she still felt for Liam, if she were honest about it, which was all the more reason to keep him at arm's length. She had made the mistake seven years ago of allowing her emotions to overrule caution. She'd persuaded herself that his ruthless, ambitious, womanising reputation was mostly the product of jealous minds, and look where that had left her. He might have mellowed a little on the surface, but people didn't change fundamentally. The way he had treated Paula Lambert was proof enough of that.

In any case, there was Jamie to consider. Better no father at all than a reluctant one—who might deny responsibility to start with.

More than half anticipating some further approach, she told herself it was all for the best when she heard nothing more from him over the following few days. Life went on much as it had before, with work taking up the greater part of it. After one further, tentative enquiry, Hugh took the hint and let the subject drop. Her business was her business.

The weekend came round again, this time with no Friday soirée to dress for. Regan took Jamie to the local park to play on the swings and roundabouts for half an hour or so, returning home to a couple of games of Scrabble before tucking him into bed around eight-thirty.

Sarah came up with a bottle of wine. Don had gone out for a drink with a pal, she said, so why not follow suit? They drank a couple of glasses apiece, and enjoyed an undemanding hour talking about whatever came to mind. By the time they parted, Regan was feeling more than a little elevated.

It wasn't yet ten o'clock, she saw in some surprise. The night was still young! So what? asked the voice of reason, bringing her sharply down again from the heights. So what indeed?

Early as it was, she might as well go to bed, she decided. At least there was the weekend to look forward to, although she'd have to cudgel her brains to find something different to do on Sunday. They'd just about exhausted the affordable pastimes.

She was about to pull out the sofa bed when the doorbell rang. Sarah must have forgotten something, she thought, going to open the door. A joke about the effects of too much wine ready on her lips, she froze in suspended animation for a moment on seeing who the caller was, catching up with a painful jolt as her heart regained its rhythm.

'How did you get in?' she demanded.

'The usual way,' Liam answered. 'The outside door wasn't completely closed.'

Don! she thought. He'd been careless before. Not that it mattered at this particular moment who had left the door open.

'What do you want?' she asked, knowing it a pretty stupid question.

His brief smile suggested a similar assessment. 'I tried staying away. It didn't work. I had to see you again.'

'So, you've seen me,' she retorted, hardening herself against the sudden temptation to let matters take their own course. 'You know the way out.'

He stuck a foot in the door to keep it from closing. 'Stop playing the hard case. It isn't the way you feel.'

'You'd know, of course!' She was fighting to stay in control—reminding herself of the child asleep in the next room. 'Always so sure!'

'Sure I'm not going to give up on you without a hell of a lot more effort,' he said. 'Are you going to let me in, or do I have to apply pressure?'

'It's late.' She was beginning to lose her grip on the situation. 'I—'

'It's only a little after ten. Having got this far, I don't intend leaving without having my say, so you may as well reconcile yourself.'

Her eyes held his for several heart-racing seconds before finally giving way. Jamie had been really tired, Regan reassured herself. He wouldn't waken up.

'You won't be here long,' she said flatly, opening the door wider.

He made no answer to that. Closing the door as he advanced into the room, she turned to face him, striking the same semi-defensive attitude as on that previous night. 'So?'

There was no verbal answer to that either. He simply moved the couple of steps that brought him back to where she stood and pulled her into his arms.

The kiss blew her away in its emotive power, stripping her mind of everything but the desire for it never to end.

She clung to him, lips moving beneath his, body seeking the heat and hardness it remembered so well and had craved for so long. The buttons of her blouse gave easily to the supple fingers; she drew in a shuddering breath at the feel of those same fingers on her bare skin, her nipples springing to vibrant life.

'Lovelier than ever,' he murmured. 'So smooth and firm!' He lowered his head to put his lips where his fingers had been, sending wave after wave of tremoring sensation through her.

Sanity returned like a stone dropped from a height as he sought the fastening of her skirt. This was all he wanted from her. All he had ever wanted from her! The swift raging anger was as much against herself for her weakness as him for his assumption.

'Get away from me!' she spat. 'Just get away!'

Considering his obvious arousal, it was to his credit that he released her immediately. Face tense, eyes fired by warring emotions, he stood back.

'My apologies. I let myself be carried away a little.'

Fingers trembling, Regan adjusted her bra and rebuttoned her blouse. A little! That had to be the understatement of the year! If she hadn't pulled him up he would have taken her right there and then.

'I have to take my share of the blame,' she said, unable to bring herself to look at him directly. 'I was carried away for a moment too.'

It had been a great deal more than a momentary lapse, he could have pointed out with truth, but he didn't. 'So what now?' he said instead. 'Do I walk out of that door and deny us both the chance to get it together again, or do we start over from scratch?'

With what aim? she wanted to ask, except that she already knew the answer. Long- or short-term, an affair was all he would have in mind.

'I think you'd better just go,' she said huskily. 'You should never have come.'

'Why?' The grey eyes pierced her through. 'What are you afraid of?'

'I'm not afraid, just not prepared to let you into my life again.' Regan fumbled for the door handle at her back. 'I'm sure you're not short of other…entertainment.'

Liam made no move. Standing there, tall, lean and devastating in the dark blue suit, he made her long. Her jaw ached with the effort of keeping her chin up.

'You think sex is all I'm interested in where you're concerned?' he said.

'Was it ever anything else?' she challenged. 'You certainly never had any intention of marrying me. What you saw was a virgin ripe for the plucking!'

Liam made an abrupt gesture. 'I didn't know you were a virgin before I—'

'You knew. Right from the moment you first kissed me you knew!' Despite all she could do to control it, her voice had acquired a tremor. 'I saw it in your eyes—that yen all men have to be the first.'

'It didn't stop you from carrying on,' he returned hardily.

'I didn't want to stop. For the very first time since—' She broke off, catching her lip between her teeth. 'It hardly matters now.'

Liam regarded her in silence for a long moment, eyes thoughtfully narrowed. 'There's something you're not telling me,' he said at length.

'There's a whole lot of things I'm not telling you,' she responded. 'I want you out of here, Liam. Now!'

He shook his head. 'Not until you can convince me you really mean it.'

With her back against the door, she had nowhere to go to avoid him. This time she kept her lips closed when he kissed her, but there was no closing out the desire still roaming loose from the first time. It gathered like a storm, sending signals to every part of her body, building by the second to insupportable strengths.

It took the sound of a door opening to bring her crashing back to reality, but nowhere near fast enough to avert disaster.

'What,' demanded a fierce little voice, 'are you doing with *my* mummy?'

CHAPTER THREE

Liam's head jerked sharply round, face registering an all too swift comprehension as they surveyed the diminutive, pyjama-clad figure.

'I was kissing her,' he said with remarkable equanimity in the circumstances, allowing Regan to slide from his grasp.

'Why?' Jamie interrogated.

Liam shot a brief, searing glance at Regan. 'It's what people do when they haven't seen one another for a long time. Your mummy and I are old friends.'

'It's late at night,' Jamie pointed out, in no way pacified by the answer. 'I read the time on my clock.'

'It's all right, Jamie.' Regan made a valiant effort to sound calm and collected. 'Mr Bentley was just leaving.'

Liam spoke quietly but with unmistakable resolution. 'Not yet. We've a lot of things still to discuss. Your mummy is safe with me, I promise you,' he added to the boy. 'We're just going to talk.'

'It's all right,' Regan repeated as Jamie looked undecided. 'Really it is. You go on back to bed, or you're going to be too tired to go swimming in the morning. I'll come and tuck you in again.'

Obviously still a little doubtful, he turned back into the bedroom. Regan followed him without glancing at Liam, playing for time in which to sort out exactly what she was going to say. Not that there was a great deal she could tell other than the truth.

41

'Did you like kissing that man?' Jamie asked unexpectedly as he slid into the bed.

'Not nearly as much as I like kissing you,' Regan responded with forced lightness, popping one on the end of his small nose and drawing the usual grimace.

'I'm six, not a baby!' he protested indignantly. '*I* don't like being kissed!'

'You'll change your mind one day.' She pulled the duvet up and around him. 'When you're grown-up and start meeting girls.'

'Girls!' He pulled another face. 'They're rubbish!'

'You'll change your mind about that too.' She ruffled his hair in lieu of another kiss, unable to stretch the interlude any further. 'Sleep tight.'

'Mind the bugs don't bite,' he murmured, eyes already closing.

Bugs would be a doddle compared with what she faced out there, she thought ruefully. If only she'd never gone to that damned party in the first place!

Liam was still on his feet when she went through. The expression on his face was no comfort at all.

'You were going to let me go without ever knowing he existed!' he accused. 'My own son!'

'What makes you so sure he's yours?' Regan demanded instinctively.

His lip curled. 'How old is he? Six? Makes the chances of his being anyone else's pretty unlikely. Unless you took up with somebody more or less immediately after we parted.' He gave another grim smile at the look on her face. 'I guess not.'

'So he's yours,' she said. 'It doesn't change anything. If you—'

She stopped right there, voice drying in her throat as fury swept the lean features.

'I discover I have a six-year-old son and it doesn't *change* anything!' he exclaimed. 'What the hell do you think I'm made of?'

'I only meant you don't have to feel in any way obligated,' she got out. 'I want nothing from you. I didn't even want you to know about him.'

Anger gave way to scepticism, no less withering in impact. 'So why tell Paula about him in the first place?'

Regan made a small, helpless gesture. 'It wasn't intentional, believe me. I was... I needed...' Her voice trailed away again as she acknowledged the impossibility of explaining just what she had felt at that time. 'It just happened,' she finished lamely.

'Of course. Just pure spur of the moment!'

The irony spurred her flagging spirit, lifting her chin and bringing the light of battle back to her eyes. 'If I was that keen to have you know about Jamie, why didn't I let you discover the truth right away when you followed me back here?'

'Probably because by then you'd begun to realise what you might be letting yourself in for.'

'I already told you—'

'I know what you already told me,' he cut in. 'It isn't your decision to make. Not any more.' He drew a long slow breath, bringing both voice and demeanour under control. 'Accepting that it happened, what I don't find easy to understand is *how* it happened when we were both of us taking precautions.'

'I lied about that,' she admitted. 'I thought it was enough that you did.'

'Obviously you were wrong.' He viewed her dispassionately. 'Why didn't you tell me you were pregnant?'

Regan stuck both her hands in the pockets of her wrap to stop them from shaking, willing herself to look him directly in the eye. 'For what purpose? So that you could offer to pay for an abortion?'

'Don't you dare—' He broke off, shaking his head as if in repudiation of what he'd been about to say. 'There'd have been no question of abortion.'

'You'd have offered to marry me?'

'Of course.'

It was Regan's turn to curl a lip. 'Under duress? No thanks!'

'It wouldn't have—' He broke off again, jaw tense. 'There's little point in going over old ground. What we have to decide is where we go from here.'

'Nowhere!' she said with force. 'I've managed fine up to now. I'll carry on doing it without any help from you!'

There was no sign of the relief she still more than half anticipated in the grey eyes—more a firming of purpose. 'If that child through there is mine, I'm sure as hell not going to stand back and let you get on with it!'

'The operative word being *if*,' she snapped back, stung by his use of it. 'What actual proof do you have when it comes right down to it? He doesn't even look like you!'

'No, he looks like you, but the timing still applies.'

'Providing I didn't go off on the rebound, as you suggested I might have.'

A muscle jerked as his teeth came together. 'Cut it out! You didn't have it in you. Has it occurred to you that you've robbed him as well as yourself these past years?'

That pulled her up as nothing else could have done. Jamie had never been a deprived child in the basic sense, but there was no doubt that both in financial and emotional terms, he had lacked a father's input.

'I suppose, if you want to contribute to his upkeep from now on, I can hardly refuse,' she said stiffly. 'But that's as far as it goes.'

'No way.' Liam hadn't raised his voice but there was no doubting that he was adamant. 'I may have missed the first six years of his life; I can at least have some say in the rest.' He winged another glance about the room. 'This is no place to bring up a child in. He needs somewhere to play, for a start.'

'There's a park within walking distance.' Regan couldn't completely eradicate the defensive note from her voice. 'We go there every weekend. And he gets plenty of exercise at school.'

'How about holidays? I don't imagine you can afford to take more than the statutory time off from your job.'

'I pay Sarah from the flat downstairs to look after him when I can't be here. She's very reliable—and she thinks the world of him.'

'I'm sure of it. It's still a long way from an ideal situation.'

Regan studied the taut features, vainly trying to read the mind behind the grey eyes. 'What exactly are you suggesting?'

'We obviously need to talk things through.' Liam made a decisive movement. 'Only not now. We both need time to consider. I'll come back in the morning. Say nine-thirty.'

Short of packing their bags tonight and taking off for somewhere he wouldn't be able to find them, there was nothing Regan could do but accept. 'I suppose so,' she said reluctantly. 'Although Jamie is going to hate missing his swimming lesson.'

'He can go later.' There was a momentary pause as he regarded her, eyes shuttered against her. 'You'd better get some sleep. You look exhausted.'

Hardly surprising, she thought, doubting that sleep would be forthcoming with so much going on in her mind.

She watched him walk to the door, torn between conflicting emotions as he turned for a final word.

'Nine-thirty,' he repeated. 'Be here.'

'Do I have any choice?' she asked.

'None,' he confirmed. 'From now on, it's a dual concern.'

Duel might be a more appropriate term, came the thought as the door closed in his wake. She had opened up a regular can of worms with that unthinking retort to Paula Lambert's harassing.

Or had it really been so unthinking? queried the small inner voice. Wasn't it just remotely possible that deep down she had wanted Liam to know about Jamie? Possible even tonight, in fact. He wouldn't have forced his way in if she'd shown any positive rejection.

Regardless, she had made her bed and now must lie on it, because he wasn't going to back off for certain.

Only neither was he going to take over in any fashion, she vowed. Jamie was *her* son. She would have the last word regarding his future.

She did sleep in the end, but was awake again at six, with no desire to make any further attempt to doze off. Jamie slept through to his usual seven, emerging in his pyjamas to cast a suspicious glance about the living room as if in anticipation of seeing last night's visitor lurking somewhere.

'He went home hours ago,' Regan assured him. She hesitated before adding to the statement, aware that she was going to have to tell him the truth but not at all certain, even now, just how to put it. 'He's coming back this morning to talk to us both,' she said at length.

Jamie looked puzzled. 'Why?'

Regan drew a long slow breath and decided that the

only way to deal with this was openly and honestly. 'He's your daddy,' she said.

'I don't have a daddy,' came the response. 'He went away when I was a baby.'

'That's what I told you.' She drew the diminutive figure to a seat on the now made-up sofa, resisting the urge to put her arms about him and tell him to forget the whole thing. 'It was wrong of me to let you think he'd deserted us. The truth is that he never even knew about you.'

Green eyes regarded her unblinkingly. 'Why didn't he know about me?'

'Because I didn't tell him you'd been born.'

Jamie digested this in silence for a moment, never taking his eyes from her face. 'Why didn't you tell him?'

'Because I believed he wouldn't want to know.'

'But he found out about me?'

'Yes.' There was no reason, Regan decided, to go into the way that knowledge had been acquired. 'And now that he has...' she swallowed on the hard lump in her throat '...he wants to be your daddy and look after you.'

Alarm leapt in the small face. 'Instead of you?'

'No, of course not.' Regan made haste to despatch any such notion. 'We'll still be together, as always. It's just that there'll be more money to spend, that's all.'

'We've got lots of money already,' came the loyal response. 'We don't need any more. And I don't want a daddy!' he added with an insistence that reminded Regan only too forcefully of the very man he was rejecting.

'You will once you get to know him.' She did her best to sound positive and reassuring. 'He's looking forward to getting to know you.'

Jamie looked unconvinced. 'I'm going to get dressed,' he said abruptly, sliding to his feet. He went to the bed-

room door, pausing to glance back as the thought struck
him. 'What about swimming?'

'We can go this afternoon.'

'There isn't a children's session in the afternoon,' he
pointed out. 'And you always said it was too busy.'

'I think we can put up with it for once.' Regan donned
a determinedly up-beat tone. 'What would you like for
breakfast?'

Temporarily side-tracked, Jamie took little time to consider. 'Cornflakes with a banana sliced on top, and a
boiled egg with soldiers, please.'

At least his appetite remained unimpaired, thought
Regan in some relief. Thankfully he appeared to have in-
herited her metabolism and remained a normal weight for
his age no matter how much he ate.

She went to start preparing the meal as he disappeared
back into the bedroom, refraining from reminding him to
wash his ears as well as his face, as she usually did. He
had quite enough to be going on with—a great deal more,
in fact, than any six-year-old should be expected to take
in their stride. This meeting with his father was going to
be no picnic for any of them.

Liam arrived promptly on the half-hour. Dressed casually this morning, in jeans and light sweater, he looked
in total command of himself.

'Hi again, Jamie,' he said easily, undaunted, on the surface at least, by the child's unsmiling regard.

'Mummy says you're my daddy,' was the stony response, 'but I don't like you!'

'You don't know me yet.' Liam maintained the same
easy tone. 'That's a matter we have to rectify. I thought
we might all go to the swimming baths together, by way
of a start.'

'I missed my lesson,' Jamie responded, unimpressed by the offer.

'I phoned the local centre and rebooked you for the ten-thirty session,' his father returned and this time gained a perking of interest. 'It's the same teacher you always have. He seems very pleased with your progress, by the way.'

'I can swim a hundred metres,' Jamie declared with some pride. 'I've got a certificate.'

'That's more than I can say.'

'Can't you swim at all?'

'Well, yes, but I don't have any awards for it.'

'*I'm* going to swim in the 'Lympics when I'm old enough!'

'*O*lympics,' Regan corrected automatically.

'*O*lympics,' Jamie repeated, placing the same emphasis on the first syllable. He switched his attention back to his father, by no means completely won over but with resolve visibly weakening. 'You won't be able to come in the water too.'

'I know,' Liam agreed. 'It will give your mummy and me time to talk while we watch you.'

'Do you really think it the time and the place?' asked Regan shortly, feeling more than a little left out.

'As good as any we're going to get,' he said. 'We'll leave the car here and take a taxi. Save finding a parking space. If the centre's restaurant is any good, we can have lunch there.'

Wearing jeans and blue cotton shirt herself, Regan momentarily contemplated changing into something a little more dressy, then ridiculed herself for the notion. She wasn't out to impress Liam in any way. His interest now lay only in his son.

'It's okay,' she confirmed. 'We usually have breakfast there after the early session.'

'Fine. I'll order the taxi, then. It shouldn't take us more than ten minutes to get there.'

Jamie went to get his swimming things together. Murmuring something about getting herself ready, Regan retired to the bathroom, closing the door between them and leaning against it for a moment to steady her nerves. So far, Liam hadn't put a foot wrong. If he kept this up he was going to have Jamie eating out of his hand before the day was out. After six years of her son's undivided love, she wasn't sure how she felt about sharing him in any fashion.

Downright unwilling, if the truth were known, she admitted. Accepting money from Liam in order to enhance Jamie's lifestyle was one thing, having him take a hand in any aspect of his day to day upbringing quite another.

Still, it would hardly come to that, she assured herself. All Liam wanted was to allay the guilt he so obviously felt over abandoning her in the first place. Once he had the financial side settled he would no doubt be content to fade into the background. After all, he had his own life to lead. One in which a child would play little part, she was certain.

He was perched on a chair arm reading the certificate Jamie had brought out to him when she emerged from the bathroom.

'Very impressive,' he declared, rerolling the parchment to hand it back to the boy. 'You should have it framed to hang on the wall.'

'We're going to do that,' claimed Regan swiftly, kicking herself for not having got around to it before this. 'Along with all the others he's going to get.'

'Too right.' Liam came to his feet, taking in the freshly

applied lipstick with a tilt of eyebrow. 'All ready? The taxi should be here any minute.'

'All but my jacket and bag,' she confirmed. 'They're in the bedroom.'

'There's only one wardrobe, so we have to share it,' Jamie advised. 'Mummy doesn't have as many clothes as I do, though.'

'Quality rather than quantity,' Regan claimed without haste. 'I like things to last.'

'You always had good taste,' Liam observed.

'Not in everything,' she flashed back before she could stop herself, and saw his jaw firm again.

'I said taste, not sense. There's a difference.'

There was indeed, she reflected wryly. Getting at him that way was a waste of time and breath when it was all so far in the past.

A ring on the outer doorbell heralded the arrival of the taxi-cab. Regan donned a lightweight windcheater and snatched up the stylish backpack she had picked up for a song at a local bring-and-buy, then went to accompany father and son downstairs.

Sarah opened her door at the sound of descending feet, her glance going from the child to each of the two adults at his back in surprised speculation.

'I was just about to slip up to make sure you were both all right after not going out for your usual bus,' she said. 'I didn't realise you had a visitor.'

'You must be Sarah,' said Liam before Regan could speak. 'I'm Liam Bentley, Jamie's father. I want to thank you for the care you've taken of him.'

Sarah murmured something about it being a pleasure, returning indoors looking thoroughly dazed.

'I'm going to have some explaining to do,' commented Regan ruefully as they left the house.

'Only as much as you see fit,' Liam returned. 'It's no one's business but your own.'

Traffic proved surprisingly light for a Saturday morning. Jamie went straight off to get changed on reaching the sports centre, leaving the two of them to make their way up to the viewing balcony running around three sides of the pool.

The children were already gathering for their lesson, supervised by the man Regan had come to know quite well over the last year. He lifted a hand in greeting on seeing her take a seat. Someone else who would be wondering where Jamie's father had been all his life, she reflected. All very well for Liam to say she owed no one any explanations.

Jamie put in an appearance, not in the least put off his stride by joining a group of strangers. Swimming was a serious business in his view. He gave it all his concentration.

'He's a great kid,' Liam declared. 'You've done a good job.'

'Considering,' she finished for him.

He shook his head. 'I wasn't even thinking of qualifying it. It can't have been easy.'

'It wasn't,' she acknowledged. 'But I wouldn't have missed it.' She turned her head to look at him directly, pulse rate increasing as she viewed the firm masculine features, the tan of his skin enhanced by the whiteness of his sweater. 'It must have been a real shock for you when he appeared last night.'

'You could say that.' He was giving little away. 'Why did you try denying he was mine?'

Regan lifted her shoulders. 'A last-ditch attempt to keep things the way they were before I let my mouth run away with me, I suppose. If that woman hadn't been so damned…' She let it lie, mouth rueful. 'No excuse. I should have just walked away the way you did.'

'And left her to stew!' Liam gave a short laugh. 'That would have been really cruel.'

'I hear she gave you a pretty hard time.'

'You could say that.'

She should feel guilty, Regan supposed, for being the one to set that particular scene, but she didn't. 'Oh, well, as you said the other night, you wanted out, anyway,' she remarked. 'Not that I see you having any difficulty breaking things off.'

'So *you* said the other night.' Liam made a dismissive gesture. 'Forget Paula. We've more important things to discuss.'

Regan turned her attention back to the pool below, where the children were just about to start their individual dives into the water. 'I'll be grateful, of course, for any help you care to give,' she said, 'but I—'

'But you're not prepared for any further input on my part,' he interjected. 'Sorry, I can't accept that. I've a lot of lost ground to make up.'

Regan was silent for several moments, face still averted. He meant with Jamie, of course, not her. Last night's episode had meant nothing beyond what she'd taken it to be—a yen to renew his acquaintance with her body. A matter of importance to him no longer, it seemed.

'Exactly what kind of arrangement do you have in mind?' she asked hollowly.

'One we all of us might benefit from,' he said. 'First and foremost, I think you should meet my daughter.'

That brought her head back round—sharply enough to jerk a small cry from her lips as pain shot through her neck. 'I must have trapped a nerve,' she said in response to Liam's look of concern. Rubbing the spot, she viewed him uncertainly. 'Your daughter?'

'Four years old,' he confirmed. 'Her name's Melanie. Goes well with Jamie, wouldn't you say?'

'How's your wife likely to react to the news that you have a son too?' asked Regan, still too taken aback to think straight.

'Ex-wife.' He gave a brief shrug. 'It's unlikely she'll ever know about it. I haven't seen her in four years. Neither has Melanie.'

Green eyes darkened as the import struck home. 'You mean she deserted her own child?'

'In a nutshell.' His mouth twisted. 'Not all women have a natural mothering instinct.'

'Then, why—?'

'One of the tricks Nature tends to play. Andrea had no desire for children. If I hadn't put a stop to it, she'd have had an abortion. As it was, she took off at the earliest opportunity after Mel was born. She's somewhere in the States now.'

'Married again?' Regan ventured.

'I've no idea—and even less interest. Marrying her was the biggest mistake I ever made.'

The words were out before she could stop them. 'Give you a bad time, did she?'

'Probably no more than I merited,' he returned levelly. 'The only reason I considered marriage at all was to fast-track my career. Chantry's held the view that a suitable partner was an asset to executive staff.'

'And I wasn't it,' Regan said softly.

The grey eyes remained steady. 'You were too young—too inexperienced. Andrea moved in the same circles. She knew what was required.' He firmed his jaw. 'Anyway, it's all in the past. So far as I'm concerned now, she's as good as dead.'

Regan couldn't blame him for feeling that way. The marriage might not have been made in heaven, but what kind of woman could walk out on her own baby?

'So who looks after Melanie for you?' she queried.

'She lives with her grandparents. I spend as much time as possible with her, but it's far from the kind of situation I'd prefer. My mother's beginning to find it a bit of a strain too. Keeping a lively four-year-old entertained is no easy task, as I'm sure you already know.'

'Actually, Sarah bore the brunt of it before Jamie started school. Still does in the holidays.'

Liam regarded her pensively. 'You'd have preferred to stay home with him full-time yourself?'

'Well...yes. Only I needed to work to provide a bit better lifestyle for him than I could on State allowances.'

'You don't need to defend yourself,' he said. 'You've done the best you can for him.'

Though nowhere near what he, as Jamie's father, could and would have done had he only known; he didn't need to say it. If she had told Liam she was pregnant and he'd married her, as he'd said last night he would have done, then his life might have been very different too. It could even have worked out.

'I hate to think what your mother would say if you turned up with a son she doesn't even know about in tow,' she said, putting the thought firmly aside. 'Better, surely, if it remains between the two of us.'

'Not if we're to do what I'm planning on doing,' came the steady reply.

Bringing them back to square one, Regan reflected. 'Which is what, exactly?' she repeated.

'I think we should get married.'

CHAPTER FOUR

How long she just sat there staring into the enigmatic grey eyes, Regan had no idea. Seven years ago she would have given the earth to have him say the words he'd just trotted out so casually. Now, she wasn't sure *what* she felt.

'Just like that?' she managed at length.

'Not *just* like that, no,' he said. 'I've had all night to think about it. Two children, each minus a parent. What better solution? You could give up your job and concentrate on being a mother, the way you always wanted to do.'

'For my own child, not some other woman's!' Anger was growing in her, born of a pain she wasn't yet ready to acknowledge. 'If your mother can't cope any longer, hire a nanny. You'd find it a great deal cheaper in the long run!'

'Nannies can't provide family stability,' Liam returned. 'Mel needs a mother the same way Jamie needs a father. You'd hardly be losing out yourself either.'

'Oh, I'm sure I wouldn't!' Regan made an effort to stop her voice from revealing too much of what was going on inside her. 'From rags to riches in one easy step—the only requirement: a mothering instinct!'

'Not the only one by any means.' Liam hadn't altered his tone. 'We proved last night that we still have something going for us. Given the opportunity, we might even fall in love again.'

'Again!' This time she was unable to keep emotion at

bay. 'You didn't know the meaning of the word first time round!'

The dark head inclined. 'Whatever, our feelings aren't the most important factor at present. The childrens' needs take priority. If you refuse to go along with what I'm proposing you'll be depriving them both.'

Regan bit her lip, aware of being put in a dilemma. Jamie's welfare was her prime concern. If she turned down this offer of marriage it would be in her own interests not his.

'You don't have to make any immediate decision,' Liam advised, watching the play of expression across her face. 'I'll take you to meet Mel this afternoon.'

'This afternoon!' Regan had a sense of being drawn inexorably down a path from which there was no return. 'Why the rush?'

'Why wait?' he returned.

'Supposing she doesn't like me?'

'Mel likes everybody. She'll be thrilled to have a mummy of her own like other children.'

'I didn't say yes yet,' Regan reminded him, still reeling from the speed of it all.

'But you're going to, if only for Jamie's sake.'

'There are times,' she retorted shortly, 'when confidence can come dangerously close to arrogance! I'm not at all sure it would be in Jamie's best interests either.'

'Yes, you are. His future would be secured. For that alone, I think you'd walk through hell and high water.'

Minus love, marriage could well turn out to be the former, came the thought. Liam had already made it clear that it would be no union in name only. Judging from the response he had drawn from her last night, it would call for no great effort on her part to fulfil his needs in that direction, but there would be no depth of emotion—no real basis to build on.

A shout of 'Mummy!' jerked her out of the introspection, drawing her eyes hastily down to the indignant figure below.

'You didn't see me, did you?' Jamie accused. 'You were too busy talking to watch me dive!'

Regan had tried never to lie to him, and wasn't about to do it now, tempting though it was to opt for prevarication. 'I'm sorry,' she called. 'I didn't realise.'

Liam leaned across the rail to look down at the boy. 'My fault. How about doing it again?' His gaze shifted to the man standing nearby. 'Okay?'

'Fine,' agreed the latter. 'Go ahead, Jamie. It's clear.'

A mutinous look crossed the small face. 'Don't want to now,' he said, and jumped back into the water instead.

'It isn't like him to be peevish,' murmured Regan apologetically.

'At six, he's entitled to throw an occasional wobbly,' Liam returned. 'Maybe we should leave things for the present and concentrate on him.'

Regan wasn't loath. The situation called for more considered reflection than she was capable of right now.

Buoyed up by well-deserved praise from his trainer on completing the session, Jamie was over his huff and full of beans when he emerged from the changing rooms.

'Mr Grayson says I can be in the gala next Saturday,' he announced proudly. 'I'll get another certificate for winning.'

'Nothing like confidence,' Regan observed, thinking that was another trait he shared with his father.

'Doubt never got anyone anywhere,' said Liam. 'Who's for an early lunch?'

'Me!' claimed Jamie with enthusiasm. 'Can I have sausages and chips?'

'*May* I have sausages and chips,' Regan corrected, only realising what she was condoning when it was too late to retract.'

'We'll *all* have sausages and chips.' Liam smiled dryly at her expression. 'There are pitfalls all along the line.'

The restaurant was half empty, the usual luncheon rush not yet under way. Listening while father and son read through the menu in case there was something they both of them fancied more than the original choice, it struck Regan that anyone seeing the three of them would automatically assume that they were a family already. Jamie seemed to have forgotten his initial distrust of the man who had arrived in his life bare hours ago, and was chatting to him without restraint. Only would he be as ready to accept Liam's presence on any permanent basis?

Liam made no attempt to reopen the subject during the meal. Only when it was over and they were leaving the centre did he mention that they would be going on somewhere once they'd picked up the car.

'Somewhere nice?' hazarded Jamie, obviously not reluctant to spend more time in his father's company.

'Nice enough,' Liam answered. 'Out in the country.'

'Will there be animals?'

'Lots of them. My mother breeds Old English sheepdogs,' he tagged on for Regan's benefit. 'There's at least one litter of pups on the go right now.'

'Puppies!' Jamie sounded in seventh heaven. 'Will it take us long to get there?'

'About an hour, all being well.'

The eagerness took a slight downward spiral. An hour was a lifetime!

'Are you going to phone and let them know we're coming?' asked Regan as Jamie climbed into the waiting taxi ahead of them.

'Hardly the kind of thing to announce over the phone,' came the short response. 'Mother's shrewd enough to start putting two and two together as soon as she sees Jamie.'

'*Anybody* can add two and two together!' declared the latter, catching the words. '*I* can do double figures!'

Liam lightened both tone and expression. 'It's going to take me some time to catch up on all the things you're good at.'

Don't encourage him to show off, it was on the tip of Regan's tongue to admonish, but she bit it back. Liam was still feeling his way with his son. This was no time to start laying down ground rules.

They transferred to the gleaming Jaguar without going back indoors. Given the opportunity, Regan would have liked to change into something a little less casual than jeans, but time was getting on. Not that what she wore was going to make a great deal of difference to the way Mrs Bentley was going to view her, she reflected wryly. Especially when Liam outlined his plans for the future.

There was time on the journey to consider that future in greater depth. The temptation to just sit back and let it happen was strong, she had to acknowledge, only the pitfalls loomed too large to be thrust aside. Liam was acting from a sense of duty towards Jamie, made all the more potent by his desire to provide a proper family environment for his daughter, but was that a good enough foundation on which to build a marriage? Supposing he met someone else? Someone he could feel deeply about. Supposing she did, if it came to that?

The latter thought she thrust purposefully aside. If she went into this at all, it would be with the intention of sticking to it through thick and thin. *If* she did.

Interested in the changing scenery, and excited over the delights to be found at journey's end, Jamie kept up a chatter throughout. Old Hay, the Bentley residence, lay on the edge of a beautifully preserved village of black and white timbered cottages, the house itself a sympathetically converted cruck barn. Leaded windows caught the sunlight as they turned in through the wide gateway, creating a feeling of warmth and welcome Regan very much doubted would be borne out by the owners once they'd been put in the picture.

Liam led the way indoors to a spacious and lovely hall, fending off the enthusiastic and noisy greetings of a couple of huge, shaggy-haired canines who appeared from the inner regions.

'Pal and Peg, for short,' he said as the two transferred their attentions to a somewhat tentative Regan and a totally bewitched Jamie. 'The matriarch and patriarch of the Bentley dynasty. The others are kept outside. Most of the time, at any rate.'

'There doesn't seem to be anyone at home,' Regan ventured, sure that the cacophony of barks would have summoned all but the deaf as a post by now.

'Dad might be out; Mother will be down at the kennels preparing the evening meal. She doesn't trust the kennel maid to weigh things out properly. Mel will be with her.' Liam started towards a door at the rear of the hall. 'This way.'

The dogs accompanied them along the stone-flagged passage to a further door giving onto a large courtyard bounded on three sides by house and outbuildings. One block had obviously once contained stables, three of the doorways were now fronted by wired runs.

Jamie set off like a rocket for the one holding several yapping furry bundles, dropping to his knees at the wire to poke fingers through to the instantly interested puppies. The face he turned back to where Regan and Liam stood was lit by sheer ecstasy.

'They're licking me!' he cried. 'They really like me!'

'They're after the salt on his skin,' said Liam as the pups increased their efforts to reach the wiggling fingers.

'Don't tell him that,' Regan returned quickly, and received a caustic glance.

'I have had dealings with a child before.'

'Of course. I'm sorry. I just didn't want to...'

'Burst his bubble?' Liam supplied as she let the sentence trail away. 'Don't worry, I've no intention. Childhood's a short enough time without stealing illusion away too soon. Mel still believes in Father Christmas. Does Jamie?'

Regan gave a wry little shrug. 'He did until he started school and some know-it-all with unimaginative parents convinced him otherwise.'

'I'd as soon he didn't pass on the same message to Mel.'

'I hardly see the subject cropping up in May.'

'It will eventually.'

She cast a brief glance, responding as always to the sheer masculinity of the firm-jawed profile. 'If there is an "eventually".'

'There will be.'

'Liam!' Dressed in trousers tucked into an unpolished and obviously ancient pair of boots, with a sweater that had also seen better days covering her upper half and short-cropped hair frankly greying, the woman who emerged from a doorway further along the row was far from Regan's expectations. 'I thought I heard the dogs barking!' she went on. 'Why didn't you let us know you were coming?' Her glance shifted to Regan, losing nothing of its friendliness in the process. 'Hallo!'

'This is Regan Holmes,' said Liam before she could form an answer. 'And this,' indicating the boy still kneeling before the puppy pen, 'is her son, Jamie. Mine too,' he added without change of tone.

Faced with the same baldly stated news, Regan doubted if she could have kept a fraction of the control over expression and bearing that Mrs Bentley managed in those first seconds.

'There appears to be some explaining to do,' she said at length. 'If you'll just give me a few minutes to finish off in here first.'

'Of course,' returned her son. 'Where's Mel, by the way?'

'Your father took her with him to the post office. They should be back any minute.' She gave Regan another, very much less friendly scrutiny before turning back the way she had come.

Regan drew a harsh breath. 'There had to be a better way of telling her than that!'

'No point in skirting round the subject,' Liam answered. 'She'll have time to adjust to the idea while she finishes feeding the animals. Meanwhile, we'll go back inside and make some tea. Always a good ice-breaker, don't you think?'

The irony washed over her, tea the last thing on her mind right now. If there had been a chance of getting hold of some transport, she would have seized Jamie and left forthwith. The whole thing was impossible! Liam had to see that. He could salve his conscience some other way.

She left Jamie with the pups, confident that he wasn't going to move very far.

Equipped with an Aga cooker, and beautifully fitted in

softly glowing oak, the kitchen was idyllic. Liam filled the kettle at the tap and put it on the hob, then opened a cupboard to extract crockery, placing it ready on a tray.

'I'd never have thought you so domesticated,' commented Regan with an irony of her own.

'I even cook on occasion these days,' he returned. 'Why don't you take your jacket off and have a seat? We'll do our talking in here. The less formality the better.'

'It won't work,' she said, making no move to follow the suggestion. 'I should never have let you bring us here.'

Leaning against the work surface, Liam regarded her impassively. 'What do you find so unappealing about it?'

'Everything!'

There was a hint of sardonicism in the lift of the dark eyebrow. 'You sure about that?'

She took his meaning immediately, a flush rising under her skin. 'There's more to life than a pacified libido!' she retaliated. 'I managed fine without you!'

'Not, I hope, with my son asleep in the next room.'

The flush deepened, the anger blinding her to all but the need to hit back. 'Don't judge everyone by your own standards!'

'I don't,' he said. 'I didn't know about Jamie when I came round last night, remember?'

Regan took a hold on herself. Even if he believed her, telling him he was the only man she had ever been intimate with was too much like baring her soul. 'There was never any chance of that happening,' she said instead. 'I take my responsibilities seriously.'

'I'm glad to hear it.' He made a sudden impatient movement. 'This is getting us nowhere. If you were going to say no, you'd have done it already.'

'I'm only just getting round to considering the drawbacks,' she returned with a coolness she was far from feeling. 'I'd be little more than a glorified housekeeper when it boiled down to it. Oh, you'd be ready enough to claim your dues, I don't doubt, and after last night I'm obviously not going to try making out that I'd be all that reluctant to fulfil them, but what else would be in it for me?'

Liam eyed her narrowly. 'What else would you want?'

This had gone far enough, said that inner voice, but some devil in her kept the words coming regardless. 'A personal allowance would be a good start. On top of the housekeeping, of course.'

Whatever his true reaction, he was keeping it well under wraps. 'You have a sum in mind?'

Regret came swift and sharp. She made an attempt to rectify the position. 'I didn't really mean that.'

'Why not? It's usual for stay-at-home wives to have some income of their own. What other conditions do you have in mind?'

'None.' She ran a distraught hand through her hair, wishing to heaven she'd never begun this. 'There isn't going to be any marriage!'

His lips twisted. 'You'd deny Jamie the security it would offer him because you don't happen to fancy it yourself? Hardly the selfless mother I took you to be, then.'

'That's not fair!' she exclaimed with heat. 'It isn't a step to be taken lightly under *any* circumstances!'

'I'm not asking you to take it lightly. I'd expect commitment in every respect.'

'Which I could naturally expect from you in return?'

The sarcasm made no discernible impression. 'Naturally.'

The kettle was boiling. He turned away to fill the teapot, adding, over a shoulder, 'Are you going to take your coat off? You can hang it in the lobby.'

There was obviously no way she was getting out of here until he was good and ready, Regan acknowledged, and she was already too warm for comfort. The rear lobby had a line of hooks for outdoor wear. She slung her jacket over one of them, returning reluctantly to the kitchen to find the tea tray already transferred to the long oak table.

'Have a seat,' Liam invited. 'Mom should be here any minute.'

The definitive came easily to his lips, oddly comforting in its connotations. Regan pulled out a chair and sat, just as his mother put in an appearance.

'Your son seems quite happy out there with the animals, so I left him,' she said, directing the remark at Regan alone. 'It's an enclosed area so he'll come to no harm.' She turned her attention to Liam, who was already pouring the tea. 'Now, what's this all about?'

'Let's sit down and discuss it over a drink,' he responded calmly. 'You always did say the best antidote for shock was a cup of tea.'

'I'm really sorry for springing it on you like this, Mrs Bentley,' said Regan uncomfortably. 'I—'

'You weren't the one who did the springing,' Liam cut in. 'Not this time.' He took a seat himself, looking across at his mother. 'Regan and I knew one another before I married Andrea.'

'Not *very* long before, if I'm any judge at all,' she observed. 'How old is…Jamie, did you say?'

The question was addressed to Liam, but Regan took it on herself to answer. 'He's six. And Liam had no idea before last night that he even existed.'

'Last night!' This time, Jean Bentley couldn't wholly contain her reactions. 'But how…I mean where—?'

'We ran into one another at a business function a week ago,' supplied Liam smoothly. 'I followed Regan to her home afterwards.'

Her eyes revealed a sudden dawning suspicion. 'You followed her?'

'Personal and private reasons.' Liam kept his tone level. 'Even then, I only found out about Jamie last night when he woke up and put in an appearance as I was about to leave, so you can forget any ideas you might be formulating about my being deliberately lured. Regan would far prefer to stay in sole charge, but she realises how unfair that would be to Jamie.' He paused briefly. 'The upshot is we're going to be married as soon as it can be arranged.'

'You only met again last week!' exclaimed his mother. 'How can you possibly think about marriage this soon?' Or even at all, was the underlying intimation.

'Why wait?' he asked. 'We're both mature adults.'

Right now, Regan felt anything but. He'd said she didn't need to make an immediate decision, yet here he was taking it out of her hands. It was on the tip of her tongue to dispute the claim, but Mrs Bentley had enough to contend with at the moment. Later, she promised herself wrathfully, she would tell Liam exactly what he could do with his proposal!

'It came as a shock for me too,' she said with truth. 'The last thing I expected was an offer of marriage.'

'But one you obviously found little hesitation in saying yes to,' came the somewhat acrid response. 'Not that I can blame you. Men with a sense of responsibility to match my son's are few and far between.'

'It's not just for Jamie's sake,' claimed the latter. 'There's Mel to consider too. You and Dad have been great looking after her, but I know how much of a strain it's been at times—for you especially. Obviously it's going to take a little time to get both children accustomed to the idea of having a sibling around. Luckily they're both of them young enough to adapt. I'll make sure the house we buy isn't too far away from here so that you can see Mel as often as you like. There are plenty of suitable properties around.'

'House?' Still grappling with the urge to put a spoke in his wheel here and now, Regan couldn't repress the exclamation.

'You don't think I'd consider bringing up two children in a city flat?' he said. 'I'll get on to the agencies first thing Monday morning.'

This whole affair was fast getting out of hand, she thought dazedly. He appeared to have everything already cut and dried.

Mrs Bentley studied her uncertainly, apparently unable to decide whether her confusion was genuine or not. Liam watched the two of them, expression unreadable. It took the appearance in the doorway of an older man who resembled the younger too closely to be anyone but his father to break the silence.

'I left Mel talking pups with the youngster in the green sweater,' he announced. He smiled at Regan. 'I take it you're his mother?'

'That's right,' she confirmed.

'Regan Holmes, Dad,' supplied Liam before she could make any further observation. Not that she'd contemplated doing so anyway. Right now this was Liam's party. Her turn would come.

'Nice to meet you,' said the newcomer. 'I understand his father's here too?'

'You're looking at him,' said Liam evenly.

Like his wife before him, Peter Bentley rode the shock

with admirable control. 'He must be all of six years old,' he remarked after a lengthy moment. 'A long time to keep it from us.'

'He only just found out about the child himself,' explained his wife. 'Purely by accident, it appears.'

'Purely by accident for certain,' Regan stated, not about to let the insinuation pass.

From the look that flitted across the other woman's face, she was no nearer believing that claim, but she kept her peace.

'I'll have a cup of that tea if it's still hot,' said her husband. 'With sugar too. I'm in need of a pick-me-up.'

'I'm sorry,' Regan began on impulse, pulled up short by Liam's smothered exclamation.

'No amount of apologising is going to change anything,' he declared. 'I'm responsible for bringing Jamie into the world. That makes me responsible for his welfare from now on.'

'How do you propose taking care of it?' asked his father.

It was Jean again who supplied the answer. 'They're getting married!'

'I see.' Peter poured himself a cup of tea and spooned in sugar, taking his time as if giving himself a chance to consider his next words. 'That's a pretty big step.'

'It's the only one that makes any sense.' Liam caught Regan's eye as she opened her mouth to speak, expression challenging her to utter one word. 'From all points of view.'

'I'd better go and check on what Jamie's doing,' she said abruptly.

'He'll be fine. They both will. Mel will bring him in when they're ready.' Liam was giving no quarter. 'I'll show you round the house. Give you some idea of the kind of place we'll be looking for. If that's all right?' he added to his mother.

'By all means,' she said shortly.

Liam led the way back through the hall, opening a door on the right to usher Regan through into a comfortable sitting room. The log fire ready-set in the inglenook fireplace would be wonderful to curl up in front of on a winter evening, came the fleeting thought.

Standing with his back to the door he had closed on entry, thumbs hooked into pocket tops, Liam looked every inch the immovable object.

'So spill it,' he invited.

A stray shaft of sunlight touched the auburn hair as she lifted her head. 'I already did,' she said. 'You can't force me to go through with this, Liam. You can't force me into anything!'

'Physically, no,' he agreed. 'I'm counting on your sense of duty towards our son. He needs a stable environment. The kind money alone can't provide. Think what it would mean to him just to have you there when he gets home from school for a start. No matter how good Sarah's been in looking after him, she's still only a minder. Mel's due to start school in September too, so you'll have your days mostly free in term time. Can you drive?'

Grappling with the conflict between heart and head, she looked at him blankly for a moment. 'No.'

'It shouldn't take you long to learn. You'll need your own transport out here.'

'You're still talking as if it's a foregone conclusion,' she said jerkily.

'I'm still counting on that sense of duty,' he returned. 'Along with one or two other incentives.'

Regan kept her voice steady by sheer effort of will. 'Such as sex, for instance?'

He gave a faint smile. 'It's a factor. A very vital factor.'

'The only thing you had in mind when you came round last night, for certain!'

He made no attempt to deny it. 'Last night I was acting on instinct. It's a whole different ball game now.' He came away from the door, face registering a purposefulness that tautened her stomach muscles afresh. 'One I'm not prepared to opt out of.'

Overpoweringly male in his breadth of shoulder and leanness of hip, he came over to cup her face between his hands the way he had done that first night, holding her there for a brief moment to look into her eyes, his own reflecting a deep-down spark.

'We can make a go of it.'

Regan closed her eyes as he kissed her, willing herself to maintain some control over the emotions rioting through her, without much success. The kiss deepened as he felt her response; he lowered his hands the length of her spine to caress the firm curves, drawing her closer, moulding her to his hardening shape. There was no doubting his desire for her—if only in the physical sense. Who was to say, came the thought, that, given the opportunity, it couldn't become something more than that in time?

'You're supposed to be showing me over the house,' she said thickly, forcing herself to pull away while she was still capable.

'True.' The grey eyes were unrevealing again. 'So let's get on with it.'

The house was superb from every aspect. Regan had to admit that the thought of living somewhere similar carried not a little weight. Few women in her circumstances would hesitate to accept what Liam was offering. Even taking on another woman's child had to be made easier by the fact that Melanie could have no memory of her mother.

All the same, it was an immense decision. One she wasn't, as yet, prepared to make with any finality. Love wouldn't be the only factor missing from this marriage. Trust was another. With her and the children tucked safely away in the country, he would be free to follow the same paths he had always trodden. Could she live with that possibility?

There was another man in the kitchen when they returned there. Medium height and slimly-built, his long blond hair tied carelessly into his nape, he was one of the best-looking men Regan had ever seen, with a bone structure to die for. Around her own age, she judged, meeting the equally appraising hazel eyes.

Whoever he was, Liam looked anything but delighted to see him. 'When did you get back?' he demanded abruptly.

'Last night.' The younger man appeared anything but perturbed by the lack of welcome. 'Aren't you going to introduce me to my future sister-in-law?'

Jaw taut, Liam said, 'Regan, meet Dene.' He cast a glance at his mother, hovering in the background. 'You might have told me.'

'My mind was otherwise occupied,' she returned pointedly.

The atmosphere could have been cut with a knife. Regan looked from one person to another in some perplexity. Of all four Bentleys, Dene himself appeared the least affected.

'Obviously, Liam hasn't told you about me,' he said. 'I'm the black sheep of the family. The brother he prefers to forget about whenever possible.'

'You don't look much alike,' was all Regan could think of to say.

'Ah, that's because I was adopted. Not that it always follows, of course. Your son out there with Melanie doesn't look much like a Bentley himself.'

'Stow it!' said Liam tersely.

'Can we please concentrate on here and now?' said Jean, rallying her forces with an obvious effort. 'I…'

Whatever else she'd been about to say was left hanging in the air as the two children came bursting through the door. Dark-haired, like her father, with huge blue-grey eyes, Melanie was pretty as a picture, with a smile to melt the coldest heart. Jamie's eyes were shining.

'Can I have a puppy, Mummy?' he asked eagerly.

Regan refrained from correcting his grammar. There was a time and place for that, and this wasn't it. 'It wouldn't really be—' she began, breaking off abruptly as Liam cut in.

'I don't see why not. Only you'll have to wait until we have somewhere to keep it.'

The 'we' drew a line between the child's brows. 'It will be at home with me and Mummy,' he said. 'We can take it for walks in the park.'

'Where's your daddy?' asked Melanie suddenly. 'You said he'd brought you in his car.'

Sidetracked for the moment, Jamie eyed Liam a little uncertainly, waiting for him to confirm what he still wasn't all that sure of. Handle that one! thought Regan with some malice, resenting his assumption that a couple of kisses back there had been enough to secure her agreement.

'I'm Jamie's daddy too,' he said to his daughter. 'He's your big brother. We're going to live with him and his mummy in a new house.'

Resentment turned to full-blown anger as Regan watched the small face crumple. How could a four-year-old be expected to take news of that nature in her stride? She wanted to go to the child, to pick her up and reassure her, though that would probably be the worst thing she could do in the circumstances.

Only when she saw Jamie's expression did she remember that most of it was news to him too. He looked thoroughly confused. Turning a blind eye and a deaf ear to everyone else in the room, she drew him aside to a seat on the padded bench set against the rear wall, searching her mind for the right words.

'You'll like living in a house instead of a flat,' she said. 'There'll be a garden for you and Melanie to play in, and…'

Her voice faded as she realised the implication in what she'd said. She'd been concentrating so hard on setting Jamie's mind at rest she had totally forgotten that hers was supposedly far from made up. There was still time to rescind, she told herself, and knew she was fighting a losing battle.

'If her daddy is my daddy too, does that mean you're *her* mummy too?' he asked, brow knitted.

'No,' she said. 'Melanie's mummy went away when she was very little.'

Jamie stole a glance at the child, now seated on her father's knee, the twin dark heads close together as he spoke softly to her. 'Will you be her new mummy when we go to live in the new house, then?'

When, not if, Regan noted with resignation. 'In a way,' she said carefully. 'It wouldn't be quite the same as you and me, of course.'

There was a pause as he mulled things over. When he

spoke again it was with an element of calculation. 'I could really have a puppy?'

'I'd imagine so.' Regan smoothed her ruffled maternal feathers. Children were practical creatures when it came to sorting out priorities. 'You wouldn't mind sharing with Melanie?'

'She's just a baby,' he said with the loftiness of a whole two years' seniority. 'She doesn't even go to school yet. I can show her how do sums and things.'

Whatever Liam had said to his daughter, it appeared to have been to good effect as she was smiling again. Meeting his gaze across the room, Regan wished she could formulate the same attitude towards the affair. The way Liam saw it, the physical attraction still existing between them was enough to carry them through; she was the only one hungering for more.

CHAPTER FIVE

PETER BENTLEY'S suggestion that Melanie take Jamie upstairs to show him her gerbils was acted upon with a surprising lack of hesitation on either child's part.

'They adjust fast at that age,' he commented to his son as the two of them disappeared.

'It's perhaps as well,' observed his wife shortly. She paused, looking at Liam. 'How soon are you planning on the...wedding?'

'As soon as it can be arranged,' he returned. 'Register office, naturally. We neither of us want any fuss.'

The autocracy of it caught Regan on the raw, bringing unstudied words to her lips. 'Fuss, no, church, yes,' she stated.

The four Bentleys eyed her with varying expressions—Dene's one of amused approbation. Liam was the first to respond. 'Any particular church?'

Already regretting the hasty comeback, Regan shook her head. Taking everything into consideration, the register office would have been far more suitable. Too late to take it back now, even if her pride would allow it. She'd made a stand; she had to go with it.

'In which case, we may as well see if the vicar can fit us in right here in the village,' he said.

'And have everyone—?' Jean broke off as she caught her husband's eye. 'Why not?' she finished flatly.

And have everyone know the whole story? Regan guessed she'd been about to say. Only there was no reason why anyone else should know the truth if that was her main concern. With little outward similarity between father and son to possibly give the game away, they were simply two single parents who had decided to join forces. It happened all the time.

'We must be getting back,' she said, unwilling to face any further discussion right now. 'It's a long drive.'

'Not that long.' Liam spoke easily enough but there was a definite spark in the grey eyes. 'I'll get you home in good time to put Jamie to bed, if that's your worry. Not that one late night when he doesn't have to get up for school is going to do him any harm.'

'I think that's up to me to decide,' Regan responded coolly, forgetting the onlookers in her swift rejection of this further authoritarianism. 'He's had a very full day.'

The jerk of a muscle in his cheek was the only indication he gave of a frame of mind hardening to match her own. The forerunner of clashes to come, Regan thought fleetingly, bracing herself against any inclination to retreat. Marriage was a partnership, not a takeover. That was something he was going to have to realise and accept if they were to have any chance at all of making it work.

'What were you planning on doing about Mel for the rest of the weekend?' asked Peter Bentley diplomatically. 'She counts on her Sundays with you.'

'I thought we'd take her back with us,' Liam answered. 'We can all of us spend the day together.'

'It's going to mean you bringing her all the way back here in the evening,' his mother pointed out.

'No problem.'

In the ensuing brief pause, Regan sensed that they were all of them waiting to see if she was going to continue the argument. The children's unexpected return was a welcome reprieve.

'They want to go to sleep,' Melanie declared. 'And

we're both very hungry!' The last, on a note of plaintive appeal, drew an involuntary smile to her grandmother's lips.

'Then we'd better find something to stave the pangs,' she said. 'Did you have any special fancy?'

'Spaghetti Bolognese,' came the prompt return. 'Jamie likes it too.'

'It's my favourite,' agreed her half-brother truthfully.

'And mine,' claimed Liam. 'Must be in the genes!'

'I haven't got any jeans,' said his son, bringing a sudden sparkle of laughter to the grey eyes.

'We'll have to see about getting you some, then.'

'I've got three pairs already,' announced Melanie, not to be left out. 'One to wear, one to wash and one to keep ready.'

'Speaking of washing,' interposed her grandfather, 'I dare say your hands could do with a scrub. Supposing you show Jamie where the downstairs bathroom is.'

'Okay,' she said cheerfully. 'Come on, Jamie.'

Regan drew a small breath of relief when Jamie accompanied her without protest. He wasn't against washing in principle but generally saw no cause to overdo it.

'We may as well all have an early supper,' said Jean. 'I've plenty of sauce already prepared, and it won't take long to do the spaghetti.' Her gaze dwelt on Regan. 'That is, if you're willing to stay on, of course.'

She was left with little choice, Regan could have answered. 'It's very good of you,' she said instead, forcing a lighter note. 'Can I do anything to help?'

'You can lay the table, if you like,' came the impassive return. 'You'll find mats and cutlery in the drawers over there. I hope you won't mind eating in the kitchen. We only usually bother with the dining room when we have guests outside the family.'

A start, Regan reflected, though still a long way to go. She couldn't blame the other woman for feeling the way she did about the affair. Were the positions reversed she would probably feel the same. In fact, definitely! It was all so precipitate—so ill-considered.

If Liam guessed what was going through her mind he gave no sign of it. Both children agreed with enthusiasm to his invitation to a game of Snap. Regan could only wonder at Jamie's swift adjustment. In the space of a single day he'd been presented not only with a daddy he hadn't even known existed, but a sister, grandparents and uncle into the bargain, yet he showed little sign of the bewilderment that might have been expected. She only wished she could achieve the same easy adaptation.

'I give Liam ten out of ten for taste,' said Dene softly, leaning against the table as she set places for seven. 'You're quite lovely!'

'Thanks.' Regan kept her tone light. 'You're not bad yourself.'

'Touché!' He was grinning. 'It must have been something of a shock to find Liam has a brother he never even mentioned.'

'You could say that,' she acknowledged.

'No curiosity?' he urged when she failed to add to the statement. 'No desire to know why?'

'Naturally, I'm curious,' she admitted. 'But it's between you and Liam. If he wants me to know about it, I dare say he'll tell me.'

'Odd,' he said. 'I didn't have you down for the compliant type. Anyway, I'll save him the trouble by giving you the run-down myself. The Bentleys were close friends of my folks. They took me in when I was orphaned at twelve. Car crash,' he added succinctly.

Regan was moved immediately to sympathy. 'How terrible for you!'

'It could have been worse. If it hadn't been for the Bentleys I'd have finished up in an orphanage.' He made a rueful gesture. 'I repaid them by getting in with the wrong crowd. Finished up in a juvenile detention centre after getting caught breaking into a warehouse. Liam's never forgiven me for that. Not that we ever did get on.'

'I'm sorry.' Regan hardly knew what else to say. 'It can't have been easy for either of you.'

'No. I took off for other parts as soon as I could. This is just one of my flying visits to let the folks know I'm still alive.' He paused, viewing her with unconcealed appreciation. 'I just hope he knows how lucky he is!'

'I'm the lucky one,' she claimed. 'There aren't that many men who would do what he's doing.'

'Well, he always did shoulder his responsibilities. Just don't expect...' Dene stopped there, with a shake of his head. 'Forget it. Who am I to cast stones?'

Regan was pretty sure what it was he'd been about to say. Don't expect total commitment was probably the gist of it. No more than she'd already more or less accepted, so no point in getting uptight about it, she told herself hardily. Liam was entering into this union in order to provide a regular home life for his two children, not because he couldn't countenance life without her. The physical attraction between them might have had some slight bearing on the decision, but she wasn't going to kid herself that fidelity was assured because of it.

Liam was looking across at the two of them, his expression scarcely encouraging. So what? Regan asked herself. Just because he had a down on his brother, there was no reason why she should cold-shoulder him too. Dene might have made a mistake in the past, but he'd paid his dues. It was surely time for Liam to forgive and forget.

Helped by Melanie's irrepressible chatter, the atmosphere at table was lighter than anticipated. Liam's suggestion that she come back to town with them and they spend Sunday all together was met with excited agreement.

'We can go to Heathrow for lunch and watch the planes taking off and landing, if you like,' he went on, addressing both children.

This time it was Jamie who cried, 'Yes!'

Showing a slightly lesser degree of enthusiasm, but obviously ready to go along with any proposal that involved being with her beloved parent, Melanie inclined her head graciously. 'I'd like to go there too, Daddy.'

'Makes a change from the zoo, I suppose,' commented Dene.

Liam didn't respond. It was left to Melanie herself to say loyally, 'I like the zoo.'

Her uncle laughed. 'Just not every week!'

Liam made no effort to refute the insinuation. Regan doubted, anyway, that his imagination with regard to places to take his daughter was so limited. Dene was just stirring it. His attitude was understandable to a certain extent. He was the odd man out in this family. She felt an affinity with him on that score.

Dene was missing when they finally left at seven. Gone to see a friend, said Jean briefly. No loss, Regan gathered from Liam's lack of comment. So far as he was concerned, it was obviously good riddance.

They'd been on the way no more than a few minutes when she discovered the loss of the keys she had been carrying in her jacket pocket. A lesser man might have wasted breath on asking why on earth she hadn't put them somewhere safer; Liam simply turned the car around and headed back.

She was pretty sure she'd still had the keys on first entering the house, Regan told him, hoping she was right. The most likely place they could have fallen out was in the rear lobby where she had hung her jacket. He went to look for them while she stayed with the children strapped into the rear seats.

Emerging from one of the outbuildings, Peter Bentley came across to the car.

'Liam forget something?' he asked.

'Mummy lost her keys,' announced Jamie. 'We can't go home without them.'

'Sheer carelessness on my part,' Regan admitted. 'I should have put them in my bag.' She stirred restlessly. 'He's taking a long time.'

'It always seems it when you're the one waiting,' said Peter on a reassuring note. 'They must be somewhere in the house.'

'Either that, or—' Regan broke off at the sudden small noise as something fell beneath her seat. Reaching down, she drew a breath of mingled relief and chagrin as her fingers encountered the familiar shape.

'They're here! They must have slipped down the seatside.'

'All's well that ends well,' quoted her future father-in-law. 'I'll go and tell Liam they're found.'

Regan shook her head, expression wry. 'I feel bad enough as it is. If you'll stay with the children, I'll go and tell him myself.'

The lobby was empty. About to go into the kitchen, Regan paused as Jean Bentley's voice carried via the partially open door.

'How can you be so sure he's really yours, Liam? It's hardly as if he resembles you!'

'We might not share the same colouring,' came the steady response, 'but he's mine all right. What else would you have me do about it?'

'There are ways you can take care of him without marrying a woman you barely know! And don't smile like that! There's knowing and knowing! Obviously she's not going to say no to an offer like the one you've made her, but do you really consider her a fit person to be put in charge of Melanie?'

'As a matter of fact, I do,' Liam answered, still in the same level tones. 'Not only fit, but capable too. There aren't that many women around willing to take on another woman's child.'

'Mel's perfectly happy here with us.'

'I'm sure of it, and I'm grateful for all the love and care you've lavished on her, but it's time you had the responsibility lifted. Regan's ready to give up her job to be a full-time mother.'

'I'm sure she is. What possible attraction could a mere job hold against the kind of lifestyle you're able to provide?'

Enough was enough! Regan told herself, hiding the hurt beneath searing anger; hiding that too as she pushed open the door.

'I've found the keys,' she announced. 'They must have fallen out and gone down the side of the seat. Sorry.'

Whatever Liam's thoughts, he kept them under wraps. 'Right, then, we'll get off.'

'Who's with the children?' asked Jean abruptly.

'Your husband,' Regan answered. 'I didn't leave them in the car on their own. I'll say goodbye again, then, Mrs Bentley.'

She turned and headed back the way she had come, leaving Liam to follow on behind. Peter was leaning through the car window to talk with the children. He straightened as Regan approached, his glance going from her face to that of his son at her back in some comprehension.

'See you tomorrow, then,' he said. 'Shall you both be bringing Mel back?'

Regan shook her head before Liam could answer. 'Jamie will need an early night to be ready for school Monday morning.'

Peter said no more. He lifted a hand in farewell as the car pulled away. Gazing fixedly ahead, Regan went over the words that had passed between mother and son a few minutes ago. Liam had said nothing to which she could take exception, but neither had he claimed to have any feeling for her other than as a woman he could trust to look after his child. But, then, what else could she have expected from him? He was hardly going to claim to be madly in love with her.

If he suspected that she'd overheard the exchange he wasn't prepared to bring the matter up. He waited until both children fell asleep before saying what *was* on his mind.

'Exactly what was Dene telling you when you were laying the table for supper?' he asked brusquely.

'What *could* he have told me?' she responded equally brusquely, resenting the tenor of the question. 'Do you have skeletons in the cupboard I should know about?'

Liam gave her a swift glance that took in the high spots of colour in her cheeks, the sparking green eyes. 'Apart from Dene himself, no,' he said. 'I don't want you having anything to do with him. Right?'

Regan set her own jaw. 'No, it isn't! Not just like that,

at any rate! It's obvious that there's little love lost between the two of you, but that doesn't mean I have to be against him. He seems fine to me.'

'Oh, he would. He's a past master at eliciting sympathy.' Liam's voice was as cold as ice. 'He's also a thoroughly bad lot.'

'Because of his past? He was only a boy, for heaven's sake!'

His lip curled. 'He really got to you, didn't he?'

'I can appreciate his feelings, yes. Did you never kick over the traces when you were a teenager?'

'Not in any criminal sense.'

'Well, bully for you!' Regan caught herself up, aware of coming dangerously close to taking sides with a man she had only just met against the one she was going to marry—maybe. 'He paid for his crime,' she said on a steadier note. 'Disowning him over one mistake is surely—'

'*One* mistake?' Liam gave a grim smile. 'Is that what he told you?'

Her brows drew together. 'You mean, there's more?'

'Past *and* present.'

Thrown, she said slowly, 'Fact, or simply suspicion?'

'Past fact. Present…' He shrugged. 'Let's just say he's blotted his copybook in more than one area. Whatever, I don't want him around!'

'Your parents still hold open house for him,' Regan murmured.

'When they took him on it was a commitment for life in their estimation.' He glanced her way again, expression unrelenting. 'I mean it, Regan. You can empathise with him as much as you like, but you do it from a distance.'

Her chin lifted. 'Why would I empathise with him?'

'Rejection. You've suffered it yourself at my hands.

Hardly for the same reasons, I'll grant you, but it still creates a bond.'

'That's ridiculous!' she protested.

'Is it? You were fairly bristling on his behalf a minute ago.'

The original spark hadn't been struck on Dene's behalf, she could have told him, but what was the point? Angry as it had made her at the time, she could still appreciate his mother's attitude.

The whole affair was fraught with difficulties. Liam might want her physically now, but what would happen when that desire burned out, as it no doubt would in time? Could she really contemplate a marriage devoid of even that much passion?

'From what he was saying, he isn't going to be around for very long, anyway,' she said tonelessly.

They completed the journey in near silence. The children were still asleep when they reached Kilburn.

'Don't wake Melanie up,' Regan said swiftly when Liam made to get out of the car. 'I can manage Jamie myself. What time shall we expect you in the morning?'

For a moment he hesitated, as if weighing things in balance, then he nodded agreement. 'You're right; she needs to get to bed too. Better make it around ten.' He put out a hand as she reached for the door handle, sliding his fingers about the back of her neck to draw her round to face him. 'But first...'

Regan closed her eyes as he kissed her, willing herself not to go overboard in her response the way every instinct in her clamoured to do, regardless of her inner doubts. She needed to think—really think—about the future he'd mapped out for them all.

'It's going to be a long night,' he said softly, releasing her.

Only because he'd no one to keep him close company through it, she thought. She fumbled the door open and slid from her seat without answering, opening the rear door to unfasten Jamie's seat belt. He awoke as she did so, yawning sleepily but aware enough to get out of the car under his own steam.

Liam got out too, though he made no attempt to come round the car. 'Goodnight, Jamie,' he said.

'Night,' mumbled his son through another huge yawn.

Liam waited until they were safely inside with the door closed before driving off. Steering Jamie up the stairs, Regan wondered what the city apartment was like. Very different from this, for certain—though obviously far from the ideal family home. It was probable that Liam intended keeping it on as a *pied-à-terre* for use on occasions when he needed to stay in town on business.

Occasions when he might fancy using it for other purposes too, came the cynical reflection.

Jamie went out like a light the moment his head touched the pillow. Regan wasn't surprised. It had been a big day in every sense. She spent the rest of the evening going over and over everything. Even for Jamie, she still wasn't sure she could go through with a loveless marriage.

She had herself under strict command when father and daughter arrived promptly at ten. Even so, it was obvious that Liam registered a certain something untoward in her manner, although he made no attempt to pursue it.

Melanie was a little more subdued this morning, as if she might be beginning to realise how different life was going to be from now on. Regan could understand the child's misgivings. They were in many respects an echo of her own.

Heathrow was busy, as always. Liam parked the car in the exorbitantly expensive short-term block, and took them straight up to the roof-garden. It was a superb day, the sun high in a cloudless blue sky, the temperature comfortable. Leaning on the rail watching the comings and goings of the various aircraft, their silver fuselages glinting in the sunlight, Regan wondered what it would be like to step aboard one herself and be transported to some far-flung place. If she married Liam there was every chance of doing just that at some not too distant date.

Material assets were the last consideration, however. If she did back out, telling Jamie he couldn't have the puppy Liam had more than half promised him would be one of the hardest things, but he would get over it. Children were very resilient.

Tiring eventually of the toing and froing, the two of them retired by common consent to the playground. It was only then that Liam gave voice to intuition.

'Whatever it is that's bugging you, you'd better get it out in the open. You've been like a cat on hot bricks all morning!'

Regan kept her gaze fixed on the pair, now mingling with a dozen or more other children, intent on extracting every ounce of enjoyment from the day. 'I'm not sure I can go ahead with this,' she said unsteadily. 'How can someone like you possibly make the transition from bachelor to family man in one fell swoop? You'd be totally out of your natural environment.'

'Thoughtful of you to be so concerned for *my* well-being,' he returned sardonically.

'Mine too,' she acknowledged. 'You think the sexual side is all that matters in a relationship, but I need more than that. A whole lot more. I'd be doing neither of us any favours by marrying you, Liam. I'd as soon risk waiting for the real thing to come along.'

'I was under the impression that Jamie's future was

your prime consideration,' he said after a moment. 'You'd throw that away for the sake of an ideal?'

Way down she had been hoping for some declaration of deeper feeling on his part, Regan admitted; she supposed she should be grateful for his lack of hypocrisy.

'I'm entitled to a life too,' she claimed.

'Not at the cost of his. I can give him the kind you'll never be able to manage on your own, and you know it!'

'I'd accept any contribution you made on his behalf.'

'What makes you think there'd be any?'

She looked at him then, anger flaring. 'That's blackmail!'

There was no yielding of purpose in the set of his mouth. 'If that's what it takes. Even if you did meet someone you could really fall for, *and* who was willing and able to support you both in the same style, you don't imagine I'd simply back off and leave him to it, do you? Jamie's *my* son. That gives me some rights. We could let the courts decide where his best interests lie.'

Her breath caught in her throat. 'You wouldn't!'

'I would, and will, if I have to.' The lean features softened just a fraction as he studied her. 'He's my son,' he repeated. 'I intend doing the right thing by him, whatever the cost. If you're not prepared to do the same, you face the consequences.'

'You don't leave me much choice,' she got out, and saw a grim smile touch his lips.

'I don't intend to. Make no mistake about it, the marriage goes ahead. What we make of it is up to us.'

'Is it nearly lunch-time?' asked a plaintive little voice. 'Me and Jamie are really, really hungry!'

Liam's swift grin transformed his whole face. 'Then we'd better go and find something to eat before you both collapse.' His gaze returned briefly to Regan, challenging her to make any further stand. 'Right?'

She conjured a smile of her own for the children's benefit. 'Right.'

The restaurant was crowded, but they managed to find a table. Jamie was all eyes. He'd never been anywhere like this before. From the way in which Melanie took it all in her stride, Regan gathered that she had. Sundays spent with her father had obviously included eating out on a regular basis.

The ultimatum he'd issued upstairs lay like a pall between them. It was only because of the children that she made an effort to overcome it. Listening to Liam chat so easily with the pair of them, she envied him the ability to dissemble.

An ability that stood him in even greater stead when an exceptionally attractive, well-dressed woman about to pass their table on her way to the exit came to an abrupt stop on sight of him.

'Liam!' she exclaimed. 'How are you?'

'Fine thanks, Diane,' he answered pleasantly. 'Are you coming or going?'

'Going. Amsterdam.' The tawny eyes went from his face to Regan's and then to the two children, reaching an instant conclusion. 'You're a *real* dark horse!' she commented drily. She gave Regan a smile that held just a hint of malice. 'Have a nice day.'

She continued on her way, leaving a silence which Melanie filled with a curious, 'Who was that lady, Daddy?'

He met Regan's eyes, giving nothing away. 'An acquaintance,' he said. 'Someone I haven't seen for quite some time.'

'Why did she call you a dark horse?' the child persisted.

'She was joking.' His tone was easy. 'Eat your greens. They're good for you.'

Successfully sidetracked, she pulled a face. 'Why do things that are good for me not taste as nice as the things that are bad for me?'

'I've often asked myself the same question,' he returned. 'Much more sensible if it was the other way round.'

But not nearly as enjoyable, thought Regan. It was only too apparent that Liam and the woman who had just left had been rather more than mere acquaintances in the not-too-distant past. Apparent, too, that she had assumed a certain deception on his part. He wouldn't have been the only man putting that particular stratagem into practice by a long chalk. They were none of them to be trusted.

'When do I get to meet your parents?' he asked unexpectedly, jerking her out of the introspection and into unconsidered reply.

'I'd rather leave them out of it!'

Her tone drew a line between the dark brows, but he let the subject drop, obviously mindful of listening ears. That it couldn't end there, Regan was only too well aware. Sooner or later she was going to have to come up with an explanation. Her throat closed up at the very idea of telling him the real reason for the estrangement.

They spent the afternoon on the river, travelling up as far as Hampton Court. Jamie was fascinated by all the passing craft, large and small. He'd like to have a boat of his own some day, he said. One with an engine for preference. He was going to join the Navy when he grew up, he declared with confidence, abandoning his previous ambition to be a train driver.

'I'm going to be a sailor as well,' claimed Melanie, not to be outdone, and received a tolerant glance.

'Girls aren't allowed.'

Blue eyes flashed indignantly. 'Are too! Aren't they, Daddy?' she said, appealing to her fount of all knowledge.

'Afraid she's right, Jamie,' Liam confirmed, keeping a straight face. 'Girls are into everything these days.'

His son accepted the news with fair grace. 'You can keep my cabin tidy when I'm captain, then,' he said.

Chauvinism appeared to be bred in the genes too, thought Regan wryly. She was going to have to have serious words with him. Not that Melanie looked in any way put out by the offer. It was enough, for now, that she'd won the initial point.

An older couple nearby had overheard the exchange, and were obviously amused by it. 'You have a lovely family!' declared the motherly-looking woman. 'They get on a lot better than my grandson and granddaughter did at their ages. They were always scrapping!'

'There's time yet,' said Liam lightly.

Regan hoped not. There was quite enough contention already to deal with.

Cream teas at a patisserie concluded, so far as the children at least were concerned, a near perfect day. Regan anticipated that Liam would drop her and Jamie off at home and carry straight on from there to his parents' place, but he said he had some things to pick up first.

Instead of the modern apartment block she had visualised, home for him these days turned out to be on the upper floor of one of the gracious Edwardian town houses backing Cadogan Gardens. A lovely, airy suite of rooms, beautifully furnished and decorated.

'All done for me, apart from a few items here and there,' Liam acknowledged. 'I've no time for poring over colour charts and such. The house will be entirely down to you—unless you'd prefer to call in professional help too?'

Unable to deny a certain inner thrill at the very idea of having carte blanche, Regan lifted her shoulders. 'I shouldn't think so.' She hesitated, torn between conflicting urges, adding slowly, 'What I said yesterday about church. The register office really would be more appropriate.'

Melanie had dragged Jamie off to show him the bedroom she used when she was here. Expression revealing little, Liam gave a brief shrug. 'Let's see how it goes.'

Regan ran a hand over the smooth surface of a nearby occasional table, studying the beautifully arranged vase of flowers occupying the centre. A woman's touch for certain.

'How soon did you have in mind?' she heard herself asking.

'ASAP. There's no reason to hang around.' His tone was steady. 'Reconciled yourself to the inevitable at last?'

'You don't give me any option,' she returned, not quite able to sustain the same equability. 'I suppose I should consider myself fortunate. As your mother said yesterday, few men in similar circumstances would do what you're doing. I'll do my best to play my part.'

'I hope to arouse a little more enthusiasm than that,' he came back on a dry note. 'Starting right now, in fact. Come and give me a kiss.'

That did bring her head up, and sharply, eyes taking in the faintly sardonic tilt to his lips. 'The children...' she began.

'The children will have to get used to it some time. I've no intention of holding fire on simple impulses for fear of them catching us. You have a mouth any man would be urged to kiss regularly.' He paused, the tilt increasing when she made neither move nor attempt to reply. 'So, I'll come to you.'

Regan gathered herself as he took the few steps that brought him across to where she stood, but there was no calming the thudding of her heart, no blocking out the singing in her ears from the blood racing through her veins at the mere feel of his hands through the thin material of her blouse. He held her lightly, looking deep into her eyes for a moment before lowering his head to find her mouth with his in a soft, brushing motion that roused an instantaneous and overwhelming response.

Mind blanked, she clung to him, hands seeking the breadth of his shoulders, feeling the muscle beneath the cream silk shirt—sliding down over the swell of his biceps to draw herself involuntarily closer. His chest was hard against her tender breasts, but it was a hardness she welcomed. She wanted more—much, much more!

It was Liam who had begun it, and Liam who ended it, putting her away from him with an ironic expression in his eyes. 'One way we were always in perfect harmony.'

Regan fought to regain some semblance of control over her unruly urges. 'You mean lust?'

'If that's how you want to look at it.' He ran the back of a finger down her cheek in a totally unexpected and surprisingly tender gesture, mouth stretching afresh as he registered her reaction. 'There's nothing wrong with good healthy lust. Imagine what it would be like if you didn't fancy me at all!'

'Better if I'd never fancied you to start with,' she said incautiously, catching herself up too late as she saw the dark brow lift in sudden quizzical speculation.

'Are you telling me it was by no mere chance that you were in my office that night?'

'Of course it was chance,' Regan made haste to affirm. 'How could I possibly have known you'd come back?'

'Maybe because you'd heard I was in the habit of doing just that a couple of evenings a week.'

Green eyes held grey by sheer effort of will. 'Hardly likely.'

'Oh, I don't know. Office grapevines being what they are, all kinds of things get passed around.' Liam was smiling again, this time minus any hint of mockery. 'It's true, isn't it?'

'"The truth, the whole truth and nothing but the truth"!' she quoted with deliberate flippancy, giving up on further denial in the realisation that it was going to be a waste of time and breath. 'All right, so I planned on having you find me there. Though with very little idea, at the time, of what it actually was I was hoping for,' she tagged on wryly.

'Despite the reputation I had? Well-merited, I acknowledge.' He sounded sceptical. 'I was hardly the type to settle for a kiss or two from a lovely young thing like you. You must have known where it would lead.'

Yes, she had known, Regan admitted. Considering her in-built distrust of men in general at the time, the degree of desire for that very circumstance had amazed her too. She'd felt the pull the very first time she'd set eyes on Liam Bentley—far above her in status though he'd been back then. Going to his office that night had been the only way she could think of of making him notice her.

She could recall, as though it was yesterday, the moment when he'd opened the office door to find her seated at his desk: the slow smile as he'd viewed her...

'Looking for me?' he asked.

Already regretting the impulse that had brought her here, Regan got to her feet. 'I'm sorry,' she said huskily. 'I just wanted to know what it was like on the executive floor.'

'There's another one even higher,' he responded. 'Would you like to see that too?'

She made an effort to retain some portion of her rapidly-diminishing self-confidence. 'I don't think so. I'd be grateful if you forgot you'd seen me up here at all.'

'That might be difficult,' he said. 'You're not an easy person to put from mind. Is that hair natural?'

'Natural?' Regan put an involuntary hand to the thick tresses caressing her shoulders. 'You think I'm wearing a wig?'

His lips twitched. 'I meant the colour. It's wonderful. Like autumn leaves! You caught my eye down in the hall the other day.'

'I did?' She was captivated, even though only half believing him. 'I'm flattered.'

He laughed. 'You must be used to being noticed.'

'Not by those holding office in the hallowed upper echelons,' she returned lightly. 'I'd better go and let you get on with whatever it is you came back to do.'

The grey eyes swept her from head to foot as she came out from behind the desk, lingering on the swell of her breasts against the fine wool of her sweater for an endless moment before lifting back to her face with an expression that set her heart thudding against her ribcage. Reaching behind him, he closed the door.

'Work holds little appeal right now,' he said softly.

Regan stayed where she was as he moved purposefully towards her. This was what she had wanted, what she had hoped would happen, yet now that the moment was here she felt nothing but panic. A man of his age and type wasn't going to be satisfied with a couple of kisses; he was going to be looking for far more. The question was just how far *she* was prepared to go.

A question purely academic, she discovered within a moment of his lips finding hers. The arms enclosing her were so strong, the long, tensile fingers wreaking havoc in their feather-light movement along her spinal column. She clung to him, lips moving beneath his in growing fervency, opening to the gentle pressure of his tongue. Her whole body shivered at the silken touch on the tender inner flesh; she pressed closer to him, seeking the heat and hardness her every instinct craved for. This was how she had imagined it would be with the right man: this wonderful, overpowering emotion filling every corner of her being.

She made no protest when he urged her down onto the long leather sofa, nor when, still kissing her, he ran his hand beneath her sweater to reach the firm curves. She yearned for the feel of those hands on her bare skin—a desire gratified by the dextrous unclipping of her bra. Her nipple sprang beneath the caressing fingers, the sensation exquisite. Then his mouth was there too, his tongue a living flame.

If she had felt any restraint at all, there was no element of it left now. She wanted what he wanted: what he was making obvious he wanted. She trembled when he slid his hand up under her skirt to stroke the flimsy span of material stretched between her thighs. In another moment he would take the garment off altogether and...

The sudden buzz of the intercom brought her crashing back to earth as if from a great height. Liam, too, jerked as though he'd been struck, snapping out something low and guttural between his teeth.

'I've come up with a problem,' declared a disembodied male voice. 'I need to run it by you. Ten minutes, okay?'

Face reflecting less than charitable thoughts, Liam thrust himself to his feet to cross to the desk and depress the 'out' switch. 'Make it fifteen,' he said crisply.

Fingers all thumbs, Regan struggled to refasten her bra. She could feel her whole face burning under his gaze.

'Sorry about that,' he said with wry inflection.

'It doesn't matter.' She got out without meeting his eyes.

'It matters a great deal to me!' There was a pause, a subtle change of tone. 'We can't leave it like this. Wait for me downstairs, and we'll go for dinner.'

And wait she had, Regan thought wryly, returning to the present as the children came back into the room. Like a lamb to the slaughter!

'We'd better get moving if you're going to get Melanie home in time for bed,' she said, glad of the reprieve from further memory-probing. 'It's been a long day.'

CHAPTER SIX

HUGH received news of the forthcoming marriage with a constraint Regan felt wasn't wholly due to a presumption that their working relationship would be severed in the not-too-distant future.

'So Bentley turned up trumps,' he said. 'Some would have done a bunk rather than face up to things this way. Not that he could have gone all that far, I suppose, considering his job. One of the City's top investment specialists by all accounts.'

'You've been making enquiries about him?' she asked.

Hugh looked a little uncomfortable. 'Discreetly, I assure you. As the one who took you to the party where you met up with him again, I feel some responsibility. I just wanted to make sure he was above board, that's all.'

'What else did you find out about him?' she insisted, reading between the lines.

The discomfiture increased. 'Nothing of any great note.' He gave a sigh at the realisation that she wasn't about to accept that answer at face value. 'He's said to be something of a lady-killer. Works hard, plays hard. Nothing wrong with that, I suppose, in his position.'

'But you're thinking he might continue to follow the same path regardless.' It was a statement not a question.

Obviously wishing he'd kept his mouth shut, Hugh gave a shrug. 'You know the man. What do *you* think?'

What he meant was, could she trust him? The answer, Regan acknowledged ruefully, had to be no. Not in the sense he had in mind. A man accustomed for years to playing the field where women were concerned would find it far from easy to settle for the same one night after night—even if the will was there to start with.

'I'm doing this for Jamie's sake, not mine,' she declared. 'Whatever happens, I can live with it.'

From the expression on Hugh's face, he was as far from believing that as she was herself, but he said no more.

Back in the outer office, Regan tried to concentrate on her work, only her mind kept sidetracking. She still wasn't totally committed as yet: she still had both her job and her home. Liam's threat to take her to court over custody of their son if she refused to marry him could probably be discounted on the grounds that, unless the mother had some dire living conditions, or indulged in unacceptable activities, she almost always came out the winner in such cases.

On the other hand, she would be depriving Jamie of a life to which he was already more than halfway adjusted. His bedtime conversation last night had consisted entirely of references to the day they had spent and the ones still to come, with the promised puppy a major factor. How could she possibly tell him it was all off because she was putting her own needs first? It wasn't even as though she knew for certain that Liam would continue to follow the same path.

She was going around in circles, she acknowledged wearily at that point. Reconcile yourself to the inevitable, Liam had said last night. Right now, it seemed the only way.

He came round at eight, after Jamie was in bed, bringing with him a bouquet of red roses.

'I was going to have them sent, but I thought you'd prefer the personal touch,' he said lightly, handing them over. 'Roses for remembrance!'

'I think that should be forget-me-nots,' Regan returned. 'They're lovely, all the same. Thank you.'

'Think nothing of it.' He followed her to the kitchen, leaning on the door jamb to watch her fill a vase with water and arrange the roses in it. 'How was your day?'

Regan concentrated on the job in hand. 'Okay. How was yours?'

'Frustrating. Having second thoughts again, by any chance?'

The roses arranged, she had no excuse to linger over them any longer. She nerved herself to look him in the eye as she turned with the vase in hand, feeling the familiar frisson run the length of her spine at the very contact. 'I'm way beyond second thoughts. Did you contact the estate agencies yet?'

He viewed her for a lengthy moment before answering, appraising her feature by feature with a thoroughness that brought a faint flush to her cheeks, moving on down her slender length in the simple yellow tunic to the shapely bare legs, then back again to her face.

'I did,' he confirmed. 'I had some brochures picked up. I thought we might go through them together to weed out the dross.'

'I shouldn't have thought there was any dross in the price brackets you're considering,' she murmured.

'The asking price is no criterion, believe me.' He straightened away from the door as she moved towards him. 'I'll make some coffee—though stimulant is probably the last thing I need.'

Regan didn't bother asking why. The expression in the grey eyes left her in little doubt. He wasn't the only one suffering frustration. She'd wanted him the moment he'd walked through the door. Always had, always would, no matter what might transpire. She smothered the impulse to say she would make the coffee. He probably needed something to occupy his hands.

She had herself well in hand by the time he emerged from the kitchen with the two steaming mugs. There was no sound from the bedroom. Not that she anticipated any. Jamie always found Mondays exhausting.

Liam indicated the folder he'd tossed down on the sofa after handing over the roses. 'You'll find the details in there. There are five at present in the locality we're looking for. We can always widen the scope a little if we don't find anything worth taking a look at.'

Regan was lost on first glance through the glossy brochures. To her they each and every one looked ideal. Liam threw out two of them without bothering to read more than a few lines of the descriptive text, followed by a further two after slightly more extended perusal. The one left was stone-built and looked solid as a rock. Six bedrooms, four bathrooms, Regan noted bemusedly. How the other half lived!

The half she was to be a part of from now on, came the reminder. Lady of the manor in deed if not in mind. A whole different way of life from what she was accustomed to for certain.

'I'll arrange a viewing,' said Liam, taking her agreement for granted. 'Tomorrow evening, for preference. You can get Sarah to look after Jamie for you?'

'I'd think so.' Regan still found it difficult to accustom herself to the idea that they were going to be living, if not in this particular house, in one probably just as big and grand. 'Why would we need six bedrooms?' she asked. 'Even allowing for separate sleeping arrangements it's—'

'Separate sleeping arrangements for whom?' Liam sounded amused. 'We'll leave continental habits to the

continentals. The most nightly separation I'll settle for is
a king-sized bed!'

'I believe there's one even larger called an empire,'
Regan murmured, insides curling at the images conjured
up. 'A whole six feet wide!'

'Too much.' He put out a sudden hand to push back
the curtain of hair falling over her cheek, tucking it back
behind her ear. Regan went rigid for a moment as he ran
a slow fingertip over the very rim, her breath shortening,
pulses throbbing. She wanted to lean into that infinitely
delicate caress, to feel the fingertip on the soft skin behind
her lobe where a pulse beat so madly.

Instead, it was Liam who leaned, this time to insert the
very tip of his tongue into the pink shell, sending waves
of almost unbearable sensation coursing through her.

'Don't!' she breathed. 'Liam, I—'

'I won't go too far,' he said softly. 'Relax.'

Relax? With every nerve-ending in her body already on
fire! She ached to lie down, to pull him on top of her and
feel his weight and hardness. At this particular moment it
didn't even matter that she was only one of many he had
made feel this way. If it weren't for Jamie...

She made a supreme effort to move away from him,
thrusting a cushion between the two of them in defence.
'I said don't!' she hissed. 'Can't you take no for an answer!'

Something flared in the grey eyes, and was as swiftly
banished. 'You're right, of course,' he said in surprisingly
level tones. 'It would be all too easy to get carried away.
Seems I'm just going to have to contain myself until we
can count on safety from interruption.' He gave a hu-
mourless smile. 'Remind me to have locks fitted on all
bedroom doors.'

Her heart dropped as he got to his feet. 'You're going?'

'I've a meeting at nine. Business,' he added, reading her without effort. 'The best deals are cemented over the dinner table. I'll phone you in the morning as soon as I've made the arrangements.'

'Fine.' Regan could think of nothing else to say.

She accompanied him to the door, abased when he failed to offer so much as a goodnight kiss. All, or nothing at all, she thought hollowly, facing the empty room. So what was new?

The house turned out to be unsuitable on the grounds that it needed a whole lot of work. Structural, not just decorative, Liam pointed out when Regan ventured to suggest a professional make over. The damp course probably needed renewing, there was obvious dry rot in some of the timbers, and ceilings in several of the rooms would need replacing.

'How could the vendors contemplate putting the place on the market in that condition?' she said on the way back to town. 'And at *that* price too!'

Liam shrugged. 'It's just a figure to start at. I might have considered an offer if time wasn't of any importance. There was nothing that couldn't be fixed. As it is, we'll simply have to keep looking until we find somewhere we can move into more or less right away.'

'You'll have to do it on your own,' she returned. 'I can hardly ask Sarah to have Jamie every evening. Anyway, you're the one doing the paying.'

They were driving along a lane bounded by hedgerows that towered over the car. Liam pulled into the edge, switching off the engine with a disquieting expression on his face.

'Let's get one thing straight,' he clipped. 'I don't give a damn about the finances. What I do ask for is co-operation!'

'Sure you don't mean compliance?' Regan queried shortly.

Half turned in his seat, an arm resting along the top of the steering wheel, he studied her narrowly for several interminable seconds. 'Would this, by any chance, have anything to do with last night?' he asked at length.

Regan kept her face averted. 'You made it pretty obvious you'd no intention of hanging around without the extra stimulus.'

'I had a dinner engagement.'

'So you said.'

'It happens to be true. I came to bring you the flowers and the brochures, not with any intention of indulging myself. Unfortunately, good intentions don't always hold out so well against incitement.'

Eyes sparking, she snapped her head round. 'You're saying *I* incited you?'

'You always did.' There was a sudden hint of humour in the curve of his lips. 'Consciously or unconsciously. If I'd been able to stay on, I'd have been hard pressed to sit there all evening with that damned cushion between us! Like a red rag to a bull!'

Regan gazed at him uncertainly, wishing for the umpteenth time that she could read the mind behind those impenetrable eyes. 'If you hadn't found me...attractive still, would you have considered marriage at all?'

'Doubtful,' he admitted. 'I couldn't make love to a woman simply because she is one, and I certainly couldn't contemplate a marriage in name only, whatever the circumstances.'

His gaze dropped to her mouth, and from there down the vulnerable length of her throat to the glimpse of cleavage afforded by the deep-V-neckline of her button-through dress, taking on an all-too-familiar and heart-jerking expression in the process. Regan put up no resistance as he drew her to him. What he felt might not be love in the finest sense, but she was past caring too much at the moment.

She slid her arms over the broad shoulders, running her fingers into the crisp dark hair at his nape. His mouth was a source of endless pleasure, lips moving against hers, coaxing them apart, the touch of his tongue on the delicate inner flesh like an electric shock.

The buttons of her dress gave easily, allowing him access to the firm swell of her breasts. At the back of Regan's mind was the fear that someone might come along the lane and see them, but she was too far under the influence of those supple, knowledgeable fingers for the thought to have any real impact.

Her own hands moved without conscious volition to unfasten the buttons of his shirt and slide inside, the wiry feel of his chest hair a stimulus in itself. His skin was slightly damp, the musky masculine scent of it transporting her back seven long years.

Most of their time together back then had been spent in lovemaking. For those few brief weeks she had truly believed he was in love with her and would eventually ask her to marry him. Half a dream had to be better than nothing at all—didn't it?

'It's still early,' Liam murmured against her hair. 'We could go back to my place.'

It would be so easy to say yes, Regan acknowledged. Too easy. 'I told Sarah I'd be back by nine-thirty,' she said, drawing away from him. 'It's a quarter to nine now, and we still have miles to go.'

'If you're intending to keep me on ice till you've got the ring on your finger, you'd better curtail your own impulses,' he came back drily, watching her fumble with her dress buttons.

'It isn't like that,' she denied. 'It just wouldn't feel right.'

Liam gave a short laugh. 'It would feel damn good in my book, but I dare say I'll survive.'

He refastened his own buttons, then started the engine and put the car into motion. Regan allowed several minutes to pass before venturing to break the silence between them.

'I really do want you, Liam,' she said, low-toned. 'You can't doubt that.'

'I don't,' he responded without glancing her way. 'What women have is an infinitely greater capacity for containment. You can make it up to me when the time's right.'

Which might not be for weeks, she reflected dispiritedly. In the meantime, was he going to be content with celibacy? She doubted it. Not when he could probably have his pick of half a dozen willing bedmates!

Her suspicions were increased when he declined to come in for coffee on reaching the flats. For him the night was still young. She steeled herself to show no hint of that gut feeling when he kissed her goodnight, but there was no shutting it out. A man aroused the way he had been earlier needed some release. If he couldn't get it from her, he may well seek it elsewhere.

'As a matter of interest,' he said as she started to get out of the car, 'I contacted the vicar at St Bartholomew's and booked a slot four weeks from tomorrow. Naturally, he wants to see the two of us before the event.'

Regan subsided back into her seat, grappling with a whole variety of emotions. 'How can we possibly find a house and furnish it in four weeks?' was the first, though by no means the most important question.

'It's possible. If we don't, we'll just have to use the flat for the time being. Meanwhile, you can give notice on this place.'

'Why the rush?' she asked after a moment.

Liam viewed her with irony. 'Why drag it out?'

There was no answer to that. None, at least, that made any difference. 'The vicar,' she said with some diffidence, 'does he know...everything?'

'He does. And he approves of the steps we're taking to put things right.' There was a brief pause, a change of tone. 'I take it I'm not registered as Jamie's father?'

Regan felt her heart give a painful jerk. 'No,' she admitted. 'I put down "father unknown".'

'Then we'd better get that corrected. He becomes legitimate as soon as we're married.'

The words were out before she could stop them. 'I doubt if it will make any difference to your mother's opinion.'

Liam made no attempt to deny it. 'Maybe not immediately, but she'll come round. Anyway, it's *my* opinion that carries the weight, and I don't have any doubts on that score. Jamie's my son.'

'Mine too!' she flashed, resenting the proprietary note. 'Don't imagine you're taking over total control!'

'I don't *imagine* anything,' he returned shortly. 'Least of all a stress-free relationship. You'd better go and relieve Sarah.'

Regan went, letting herself into the house without a backward glance. Liam waited until the door was closed before driving off. Listening to the dwindling engine note, she wondered bleakly just what kind of relationship they *were* going to achieve.

There was no contact from him for a couple of days. By Thursday evening, Regan was beginning to suspect that he might have had second thoughts of his own. When he rang around eight he offered no apologies for the neglect.

'I've found a property,' he said without preamble. 'The vendors moved out a couple of weeks ago so it's minus the trappings, but it needs little in the way of redecoration—for the present, at any rate. You can make it over to your own tastes, if necessary, later.' He took her silence for displeasure, his tone hardening. 'There were others after it, so I had to make a quick decision.'

It's your money, it was on the tip of Regan's tongue to reiterate, but she held it back. 'I don't see you signing your name to anything you weren't wholly satisfied with,' she said instead.

'*Wholly* might be pushing it a bit. Let's say ninety per cent. You'll see it for yourself on Saturday.' He gave her no time to comment. 'There's going to be little time to dally over the furnishings, so I've arranged for a consultant from Gosfords to meet us there with catalogues and fabric samples etcetera.'

Regan had never heard of Gosfords, though she had no doubt that it was a very high-class establishment. Furnishing a house from scratch would normally mean trawling through dozens of stores, but not where money was no object. It was going to be quite an experience.

'You seem to have thought of everything,' she said.

'I try. I take it you gave notice on the flat?'

Regan bit her lip. 'Not yet.'

'Why not?'

'I wasn't sure you hadn't changed your mind.'

'Just because I left you alone for a couple of days?'

'We hardly parted on the best of terms,' she defended. 'How was I supposed to know *what* you had in mind?'

'You can be sure of one thing,' he said hardily. 'I don't back out on decisions once made. Tell Longmans you'll be leaving in two weeks. That will give you some time to spend on sorting out your things. Assuming the flat came furnished, there can't be all that much you'll want to take with you, apart from personal items.'

'I can't do that,' Regan protested. 'Longmans, I mean. My contract stipulates a month's notice either side.'

'Then you've already left it too late. Would you like me to have a word with them?'

'No!' She was incensed by the very idea. 'I'll handle my own affairs!'

'Fair enough.' From the tone of his voice, there was no pun intended. 'I'll see you Saturday at nine.'

Not before then? she almost asked, riven by sudden depression at the thought of another whole day's deprivation. 'Does Jamie come too?' she said.

'Of course. We'll be picking Mel up on the way. Copperlea's about ten miles from Old Hay. Close enough without being on the doorstep.'

Copperlea, Regan mused, replacing the receiver as the dialling tone signalled an end to the call. It certainly sounded like the kind of place she would like. Whether or not she was going to be living in it for the foreseeable future.

Saturday dawned wet and miserable. Not the ideal day for house-viewing, Liam acknowledged in the car, but it was needs must if they were to get it habitable in time.

'Is there a garden?' asked Jamie, priorities firmly fixed.

'Two,' confirmed his father. 'One with walls all round it and lots of flowers, the other mostly grass and trees and plenty of room to play. We'll have to get you a bicycle.'

'Instead of a puppy?' came the anxious response, drawing a smile.

'As well as. You realise you'll be sharing a pup with Mel?'

'Why not one each?' suggested Regan with faint acidity. 'Pedigree, naturally.'

Liam gave an easy shrug. 'If you've no objection to double the trouble, why not indeed?'

She'd landed herself with that one, Regan acknowledged, unable to back out on the notion in face of Jamie's unalloyed delight. Poetic justice for being such an ungrateful wretch. Liam was doing everything he could to make good for past failings. It wasn't his fault that he was unable to give her the emotional reassurance she craved.

She stole a glance at the lean masculine profile, dwelling for a stomach-tensing moment on the firm lines of his mouth. It had been three whole days since she'd known the touch of those lips. Four nights of longing for him just to be there with her. The next time he suggested going to his place for an hour or two she might take him up on it regardless.

Always providing there was a next time, of course, came the deflating thought. With less than four weeks to go, he might well decide to leave it for the wedding night.

The wedding night! Even now, with a house bought and the date arranged, she couldn't convince herself that it was actually going to happen. There'd been no mention of a honeymoon, but, then, why would there be? This was no ordinary, everyday marriage with all the attendant rituals. They had a ready-made family to take care of.

'We still have to talk about your parents,' Liam said quietly, jerking her out of her thoughts. 'I want to know why you're so against contacting them.'

Jamie was gazing out of the rear window, happily engrossed in the passing scene. Regan kept her voice low even so. 'I really think that's my affair.'

'I'm making it mine.' His jaw was taut. 'Either you tell me what the problem is yourself, or I'll look them up and have it out that way.'

Green eyes darkened. 'Can't you just accept that we don't get on?' she demanded, momentarily forgetting the possibility of listening ears in the back seat.

'There's more to it than that.' Liam was giving no quarter. 'It's something to do with your stepfather, isn't it?'

'No!' Regan caught herself up, catching her lower lip between her teeth. 'Leave it,' she pleaded, lowering her voice again. 'Just leave it, will you?'

'For now,' he said.

Regan turned her head away, feeling the pain no amount of time would ever totally eradicate. It was nine years since she'd left the home where she'd grown up. Nine years since she'd last seen the woman who purported to be her mother. She'd lied to Liam when she'd told him that was where she'd gone when their affair had ended. It was the very last place she would have gone!

That he wasn't going to let the matter drop was obvious. Whether he really would carry out his threat to look them up she couldn't be sure; he might find it difficult anyway, without more detail. What really rankled was his assumption that it was his business to start with. What was past was past. That was where it should stay.

Conversation was limited after that. Regan was relieved to reach their interim destination, where Melanie awaited them in a fever of excitement at the prospect of visiting what was to be her new home.

'She's talked about nothing else since you phoned with the news on Thursday,' said Jean on a wry note. 'She wanted to start packing yesterday. We're going to really miss her.'

'It's only a few miles,' Liam said reassuringly. 'You'll probably be seeing nearly as much of her as now. Regan's starting driving lessons next week. I reckon she'll be qualified by the time we move in, so you'll be able to exchange visits.'

Regan held back on the exclamation. The driving lessons were news to her! Both necessary and desirable if she wasn't to be confined to quarters during the week, agreed, but it would have been nice to be consulted first.

With both children chattering excitedly in the back of the car, they made it to the house in less than fifteen minutes. It was set towards the rear of the two-acre grounds, framed by the magnificent copper beeches that gave it its name. Regan fell in love on sight with the ivy-covered structure, even more so with the oak-beamed interior. There was a vast drawing room, another smaller sitting room, a dining room, a huge farmhouse-style kitchen, a study, and various utility areas on the ground floor alone. Five bedrooms this time, with two at the rear that would be perfect for the children.

'Only three bathrooms?' she remarked tongue-in-cheek, turning from an inspection of the last, beautifully fitted one to where Liam lounged in the doorway. 'A real come-down!'

'We can put in another couple, if you feel it lacking,' he returned with mock seriousness. 'There's room enough.'

Regan laughed and shook her head, still not quite believing that this was to be their home.

'I gather you quite like the place?' he said.

'Like!' She laughed again. 'I love it! How can you

possibly be only ninety per cent satisfied with a place like this?'

'There's no such thing as perfection,' he returned. 'The roof needs some attention for starters.'

'Easily fixed!' Regan was not to be brought down from her high. 'I dare say you already arranged for everything to be taken care of.'

'Nice to know you've that much faith in me.' Liam glanced at his watch. 'The people from Gosfords won't be here for another half an hour. How about a coffee while we wait?'

'There isn't...' Regan began.

'There is,' he said. 'I brought in a few groceries on Thursday.'

'You think of everything,' she observed.

The dark head inclined. 'I try. We'd better check on the children first. They've gone very quiet.'

They found the two of them seated together on the ready-carpeted floor of one of the rooms they were to occupy while Jamie read from a somewhat tattered children's story book he had found, he said, in the cupboard underneath the padded window seat. He was teaching Melanie some harder words than she already knew, he advised. They'd decided that this was to be his room, and the one with the pink carpet next door hers, because pink was a girl's colour not a boy's.

'So much for political correctness!' said Regan lightly on the way downstairs. 'To be expected, I suppose.'

Liam grinned, the intimation by no means lost on him. 'Pink would clash with his hair anyway.'

In addition to both instant and ground coffee, there were several other dried goods in the cupboard he opened, milk and cream in the refrigerator. The previous owners had left a new cafetière in a prime position. A welcoming gesture on their part, Regan took it, sorry she hadn't met them.

Liam took a seat at the big central table, also left *in situ* while she made the coffee, leaning back with legs comfortably stretched and hands clasped behind his head. He'd sloughed the light rainproof he'd been wearing in the hall on arrival. In the lightweight trousers and short-sleeved cotton shirt he looked at home already, Regan thought, vitally aware of his muscular length.

The rain had stopped, she saw from the window. There was even a hint of sunlight breaking through the cloud. A lobby she had still to view gave onto the walled garden he had mentioned in the car, with flower-beds in full and lovely late-spring bloom. The gate set into the far wall afforded a sight of grassy, tree-shaded stretches leading down to what was unmistakably water.

'Is that a pond?' she asked in sudden concern, thinking of the danger to the children.

'River,' Liam corrected. 'The Thames, to be exact. It's a fairly narrow stretch here. And before you say it, it's fenced off all along this side. Providing we keep the gate over there locked, there's no risk.'

She should have known, Regan acknowledged, that he'd have taken such things into consideration. A house on the river! More prestigious even than she had believed. What, she wondered, would the neighbours be like? Not that she was likely to be seeing much of them in any case, with the closest almost a quarter of a mile away. This was far from chatting-over-the-back-fence country.

'It's all proving a bit too much at the moment,' she admitted, pouring the coffee. 'I can't get my head round the idea that we'll actually be living here!'

Liam gave a light shrug. 'It's just a house.'

'Not to me. I've never seen anything like it outside of magazines and such. It must have cost you a fortune!'

'A pretty substantial one,' he agreed imperturbably. 'And it isn't just my name on the deeds. At least it won't be once you're officially a Bentley.'

Her bemusement was genuine. 'I didn't expect that.'

'Share and share alike,' he said. 'That's what marriage is supposed to be about.' The grey eyes were steady on her face. 'So supposing you come clean about this trouble with your parents? Bottling things up never did anyone any good.'

The coffee spilled over into the saucer as she set her cup down. 'You just can't leave it alone, can you!'

'Not when it so obviously tears you apart just to think about it.' He'd straightened his position, an arm now resting on the table as he studied her across the width, the coffee ignored at his elbow. 'I meant what I said earlier. I'll get to the truth one way or another.'

Caution went to the winds in a sudden blast of fury. 'You can go to hell!'

'There's every chance,' he said, unmoved by the vehemence, 'but not quite yet. You were always reticent about your background. I didn't take a great deal of notice in the past, I admit, but this is different.'

The rage died as swiftly as it had arisen, leaving her empty of everything but the degradation contained in the memory alone. She'd never told anyone else the story, and would prefer to keep it to herself now, but she was left with little choice it seemed.

She said tonelessly, 'My mother married Gary when I was sixteen. He was ten years younger than her. I didn't like him. He made me feel uncomfortable. Always watching me, putting his arm round me, telling me I could rely on him to look after me. There were other women too. I think Mom suspected it, but she was too afraid of losing him to say anything.' She paused, swallowing. 'I suppose I should be grateful he waited as long as he did to start on me.'

The grey eyes were narrowed, a line drawn deep between dark brows. 'Start on you how, exactly?'

'How do you think?' Regan's throat hurt. 'He tried to get me into bed with him. More than once. No, he didn't succeed,' she said, answering the question she was sure would be uppermost. 'I was genuinely *virgo intacta* when I met you.'

'I know that.' Liam spoke quietly, but there was a growing spark in his eyes. 'You told your mother about it?'

She swallowed painfully. 'Eventually, yes. She didn't believe me. Said I was making it up because I was jealous, and wanted to break things up for her so that I could have him myself. She told me to get out.'

'So where did you go?' The question was soft.

'I'd just completed a college course in business studies. I used what money I had from my evening job to come to London, and was lucky enough to land a job within a few days. I eventually progressed to the bank. The rest you know.'

It was difficult to tell just what thoughts might be going through the dark head; he had his reactions well under control. 'Not quite. If you didn't go home when you discovered you were pregnant—'

'A hostel for unmarried mothers-to-be. There's help to be got in most circumstances if you look for it. After Jamie was born I moved into a council flat. Once I found a job I was able to afford another move. Not by any means the perfect place to bring up a child in, as you've pointed out, but a great deal better than the one we left.' Regan took care to keep her voice steady. 'So there you have it. Not such a big deal when it all boils down.'

'Big enough.' Liam regarded her pensively. 'You've been let down too many times. Your father walked out on you, your mother proved herself no better...and then me.'

Her shrug made light of the heartache. 'You're making amends. Jamie will have a wonderful life from now on.'

'And you?' There was an odd note in his voice, an unreadable expression in his eyes. 'Are *you* going to have a wonderful life?'

'How could I fail to have?' she said. 'A beautiful house, a handsome husband, no financial worries—it's every woman's dream!'

His lips twisted. 'Nothing else?'

From somewhere, Regan dredged a laugh. 'Oh, a good sex life too. That goes without saying!'

The soft burr of a telephone cut through any answer he might have been about to make. Reaching into the breast pocket of his shirt, he drew out his mobile phone, answering the summons with a brusque, 'Yes?'

Watching him as the caller responded, she saw his face wiped suddenly clear of all expression, the eyes momentarily meeting hers veiled and impenetrable once more. 'I'll call you back,' he said, and switched off, repocketing the instrument just as a deep chime that could only be the front doorbell rang through the house.

'That will be Gosfords,' he said, getting to his feet.

Regan accompanied him from the kitchen without enthusiasm. That he hadn't been prepared to speak to the caller while she was listening was more than evident. It could be business, of course, but it didn't seem likely on a Saturday. Which left the probability that it had been a woman on the other end of the line. A woman he would be calling back later, when he was alone.

To say...what?

CHAPTER SEVEN

ATTENDED by just a few close friends and contemporaries, the wedding went without a hitch. Regan opted for a deep gold brocade suit that could be worn later, while Liam settled for a grey pinstripe. Neither child took an active part in the proceedings, but watched from the sidelines along with their grandparents.

The buffet reception was held at the house. Sipping champagne in the cream-carpeted, beautifully furnished drawing room, Regan still found it difficult to believe that so much could be done in four short weeks. If Hugh hadn't insisted on arranging for her to leave work on one week's notice, she would never have managed to get through. He and Rosalyn, along with Sarah and Don, were the only people on her side here today.

'Liam's a lucky man,' declared the best man, raising his glass to her.

'I'm the lucky one,' she responded, returning the smile. 'Liam tells me the two of you more or less grew up together.'

'You could say that,' he agreed. 'My folks and his are old friends. We went through school and university together.'

'But you didn't follow the same career path.'

'I didn't have Liam's astuteness in the field of high finance. My bent is computer technology.'

'You have your own company, I believe.'

He gave a deprecatory shrug. 'Small-time compared with what Liam's achieved.'

'Did I hear my name mentioned?' asked the latter, joining them.

'Only in passing,' Regan returned, stomach muscles fluttering, as always, at the magnetic allure of his dark good looks. 'I ought to go and see what the children are doing.'

'Dad has the pair of them in hand,' he said. 'They're both quite happy.'

Regan didn't doubt it. The two of them had adjusted to each other with amazing ease. It was her own relationship with Melanie that caused her some concern. Try as she might, she couldn't get close. Liam would be around for the next couple of days, but once he returned to work and Jamie started his new school it was just going to be the two of them. Somehow, she had to achieve a breakthrough.

Not just with Melanie either, came the thought. The bond between her and Liam was far from absolute. Tonight they would share a bed for the first time in seven years. Whether they would still be sharing it seven years hence was another matter.

She came back to earth at the sound of her name, to find both men viewing her curiously.

'Warren asked if you rode,' said Liam.

Regan found a smile. 'Sorry, I'd drifted. No, I don't. Is it mandatory in rural areas?'

Warren grinned back. 'Some would like it to be. I'm no horseman myself, but I have a sister who'd ban all cars in favour. You'll have to meet her. You're about the same age.'

With little else in common, from the sound of it, Regan reflected. 'That would be nice,' she said politely.

'I thought Dene might have made an effort to be here,'

Warren went on, turning his attention back to Liam. 'Family occasion, and all that.'

The other man shrugged, expression giving little away. 'I've no idea where he is right now.'

'Pretty thoughtless of him, but that's Dene, I suppose.'

Close friend though he was, apparently Warren wasn't aware of just how unwelcome Dene's presence here today would have been so far as Liam was concerned, Regan reflected. There had been no mention of him since his departure the day after she had first visited Old Hay. It might be months, she had gathered from what he had told her, before he dropped in on his adoptive parents again. It was such a shame that Liam couldn't bring himself to put the past aside.

Hugh and Rosalyn were the first to leave. Their departure started a general exodus. By half past five only the Bentleys themselves remained.

It was Peter who made the offer to take both children back with them for the night.

'You'd have done better to leave the pair of them with us for a week or so and get away somewhere,' he said, 'but at least you should have a little time on your own. We'd take good care of Jamie,' he added, seeing the doubt on Regan's face.

'I'm sure you would,' she said. 'It's just that he might feel…pushed out. They both might.'

'Not according to the way they reacted when we asked them.' He laughed. 'Of course, the animals are the biggest draw. You'll get no peace until you sort out the puppy situation.'

'We will,' said Liam before Regan could respond. 'And thanks, Dad. We could use some time on our own.'

He was right, Regan conceded. With the children *in situ* they wouldn't have been able to relax—at least she certainly wouldn't. This way they could spend the whole night making love without fear of a small figure appearing in the bedroom doorway.

The whole night. Her pulses went into overdrive at the very thought. She could only hope that nothing showed in her face as she added her thanks to Liam's.

If Jean was less enthusiastic than her husband about the arrangement, she didn't reveal it. She and Regan had reached a truce of sorts over the past weeks, and she was always kindness itself to Jamie. He went off in the car quite cheerfully on the assurance that he would not only be returning the following day but going to look at puppies into the bargain.

The very first time they'd been apart overnight, Regan acknowledged, watching the car out of sight round the curve of the drive. Not the last, of course. There would be more and more occasions as he grew older. One thing she couldn't and wouldn't countenance was boarding school, though, however superior the educational resources might be.

'So what would you like to do with the rest of the evening, Mrs Bentley?' said Liam at her back.

Go straight to bed, was her prime inclination, but she couldn't bring herself to say it. If Liam was really as desperate for her as she for him he wouldn't be asking the question. She knew a longing for him to sweep her up in his arms and carry her upstairs, the way Rhett did with Scarlett in *Gone With The Wind*. He was certainly physically capable.

The caterers had already cleared everything and departed. Tomorrow, the domestic help Liam had insisted on taking on would be here to see to the house itself. Between now and then they only had themselves to please.

'Would you prefer going out somewhere to dinner, or shall I cook something?' she asked.

He laughed softly, fingers cool at her nape as he moved her hair aside. She went weak at the knees at the feel of his lips on the tender skin, the blood beginning to sing in her veins.

'It's still only early,' she murmured.

'I know,' he said.

He drew her backwards in order to close the door, turning her about to tilt her chin for a kiss that stirred her to the depths. She put her arms about his neck and returned the ardour, body moving instinctively into closer contact with his. So what if it was barely six o'clock? What if she'd barely eaten a thing since breakfast? This was the only food she needed right now.

'Dinner can wait,' Liam declared, echoing her thoughts. '*I've* waited long enough!'

He didn't carry her up the stairs, but he kept an arm about her waist. Reaching the bedroom they were to share, he closed the door and flicked the switch controlling the bedside lamps, then went across to draw the brocade drapes, creating an intimacy daylight couldn't provide.

Regan watched him, loving the way he looked, the way he moved. Seven long years since they had been together the way they were going to be in a moment or two. Seven years during which *he* certainly hadn't been celibate, came the creeping thought, thrust swiftly aside before it could penetrate too deeply.

They undressed each other between kisses—a voyage of rediscovery. For Regan it was like going back in time. The fine male body was no different from when she'd last explored it: chest deep, stomach ridged with muscle, hips lean and taut, loins firm in their enclosure of the vibrant manhood. That there were differences in hers she was well aware. Her breasts were fuller now, her hips a little more curvy, her waist not quite so reed-slender: a woman's body rather than a girl's. But it pleased him still, she could tell. Perhaps even more.

'Maturity suits you,' he said softly, cementing the impression. He cupped both breasts in his hands, lifting each tingling, hardening nipple to his lips in turn. 'Beautiful all through!'

He drew in a sharp breath as she took hold of him, closing his eyes to savour the exquisite sensation. 'Beautiful!' he repeated.

Regan tremored anew when he gratified her earlier desire by swinging her up in his arms without effort to carry her to the bed, kicking aside the scattered garments as he went. Drawing back the covers with one hand, he laid her down on the cool cotton sheet, standing there for a moment to run possessive eyes over her before lowering himself to kiss her lips, her eyes, the hollow of her throat— bringing himself gradually, oh, so gradually into full contact.

The potent pressure at the joining of her thighs brought memory flooding back full-force. She opened to him readily, her breath catching as he slid all the way inside her. It felt so wonderful to have him there again, so deeply joined together. She wanted to keep him there for all time.

Watching her face, he began to move, gently at first, then with slowly building pace and power until all thought ceased and she was conscious only of the overwhelming sensation. Her climax was like nothing that had ever gone before, drawing inarticulate sounds from her throat as her whole body arched in ecstasy. Liam echoed her cries as he too reached the zenith.

It was some time before either of them found the strength to move. Regan had the feeling that Liam had fallen asleep for a minute or two, although there was nothing sleepy about the grey eyes when he eventually lifted his head from her shoulder.

'That,' he said, 'was worth every minute of frustration I've suffered these past weeks! You're a revelation, Mrs Bentley.'

'Better than I used to be?' she asked, trying to keep the question light.

'An unfair comparison,' he said. 'You were an inexperienced girl then, you're a woman now.'

She hesitated before taking him up on the perceived implication. 'You mean I've had time to learn how to fully satisfy a man?'

His shrug was brief. 'I'd hardly expect you to have gone seven years without a man at all.'

It was on the tip of her tongue to tell him that that was exactly what she had done, but something held the words back. Why give him reason to suspect the truth—that she'd spent the last seven years pining for him?

'I'd as soon forget the past and concentrate on the present,' she said huskily. 'Can you still manage it twice?'

A devilish spark lit the grey eyes. 'Thinking I might be past it?'

He rolled onto his back, carrying her with him and pressing her upright to join the two of them together again, the hands clasping her hips holding her still for several electrifying moments of total possession before urging her into movement.

Regan had believed that first climax unsurpassable, but she was wrong. This time was beyond all imagination.

'You were saying?' he murmured some untold minutes later when she lay drained and nerveless by his side.

'Just testing,' she said without opening her eyes. 'All doubts well and truly laid.'

The laugh came low. 'I'm glad to hear it.' He added softly, 'You're a whole new character, green eyes.'

'It's a whole new chapter,' she returned.

Liam laughed again. 'Developing nicely too.' He kissed her lightly on the lips, then sat up, shoulders bronzed in the lamplight. 'I'll go and see if there's any champagne left. I feel like celebrating some more.'

He didn't bother to don any clothes; with the house empty, he obviously felt no need. Regan watched him cross the room, aroused once more by the sheer masculinity of the firmly muscled behind. That her body stirred him the same way was obvious. Only how long would it be before custom staled his appetite?

Thinking that way wasn't going to help, she told herself staunchly. It was up to her to keep his interest alive; up to her to arouse the deeper emotion she craved from him. The marriage might be largely a matter of convenience now, but it didn't have to stay that way.

She got up to run a brush over her hair and apply a squirt of perfume. Viewed through the dressing mirror, her eyes held a glow she hadn't seen there in years. She felt vibrant all the way through, every nerve, every sinew aquiver. It was still only twenty past seven. That left a whole twelve hours before they needed to come down to earth.

She was back in the bed when Liam returned with an unopened bottle and two glasses. Totally without self-consciousness in his nudity, he popped the cork and poured the sparkling liquid, bringing both glasses across to where she lay propped on the pillows.

'To us!' he said, lifting his own glass in salute.

'Us,' Regan echoed with growing confidence. Whatever it took, this marriage was going to last!

The children arrived at nine-thirty the next morning looking unusually subdued.

'They neither of them slept too well,' said Peter a little diffidently. 'You might find them a bit fractious with each other.'

Regan had a feeling there was rather more to it than he was letting on, but was reluctant to probe. He declined the invitation to accompany them on their tour of the kennels. He saw enough of puppies, he said in what she considered only semi-jocular tones. The dog-breeding was Jean's pursuit. He might lend a hand in the business, but that didn't necessarily mean he had the same overriding interest.

It must make things easier if married couples did share similar interests, though, she thought, feeling suddenly downbeat again. Outside of the bedroom, she and Liam didn't really have all that much in common. She liked walking, while he preferred to take his exercise in the gym. She was looking forward to doing some gardening, while he saw no point in grubbing in the dirt, as he put it, when they had a gardener coming in twice a week. They would be doing some entertaining once they were settled in, he had said last week, which hadn't exactly filled her with delight either. Playing hostess to his associates—business *or* personal—had not been in her scheme of things.

The price to be paid, she told herself resolutely now. A small enough return for all she had gained.

The children fell in love instantly with the litter of eight-week-old West Highland terriers Liam had already sussed out as suitable both in size and temperament. There were only four left, the two he'd put a hold on both male. Faced with Melanie's adamant preference for one of the remaining females, he gave in without argument. They could, he said on the quiet, always have the animal spayed when she reached a suitable age, to cut out any chance of inbreeding.

'Or have the dog castrated,' suggested Regan, tongue tucked only slightly in cheek. 'It's said to make them a lot more biddable.'

Liam gave her a dry glance. 'Only because they get too fat and lazy to be anything else. A dog needs all his parts to know he's a dog.'

'And a bitch doesn't?'

'Not in the same sense.'

'Typical male arrogance!' she shot back.

'You're probably right,' he agreed with maddening calm. 'We're a vainglorious breed. Do you think you'll cope?'

'With you or the pups?' she asked, and saw his smile come and go.

'You'll be seeing a whole lot more of the pups once I'm back in the fray. I'm no nine to five man.'

Regan was silent for a moment, watching the two children playing with the young animals. When she did speak it was in somewhat flatter tones. 'You didn't tell me just how far up the ladder you actually are.'

He made no attempt to downplay his role. 'Does it matter?'

'It underlines the fact that you know a great deal more about me than I do about you.'

Liam glanced her way again. 'Do you regret telling me about your mother?'

'No,' she admitted. 'It was something of a relief to let it out in the end. Not that you gave me much choice.' She paused, then added curiously, 'Would you really have done what you threatened to do if I hadn't told you?'

'I'd have had difficulty putting on a trace with only a

vague memory of you once mentioning your home town and no idea of your stepfather's name,' he admitted.

'Are you as ruthless in business as you are in life?' she asked after a moment.

'Where necessary. It—' He broke off abruptly as Jamie gave Melanie a none-too-gentle shove. 'Hey, that's enough!'

'This is *my* puppy!' claimed his son fiercely, clutching the wriggling little form to his chest. 'She's got one of her own!'

'I only wanted to look,' declared the younger child on a plaintive note. 'He's being mean to me again, Daddy!'

Dark brows drew together as his gaze went from her face to Jamie's defiant one. 'Again?'

Had there been any doubt as to his parentage, the resemblance between boy and man was indisputable at this moment, thought Regan fleetingly, viewing the set of the small jaw line, the tilt of the bright head.

'He said boys are better than girls,' Melanie proffered when it became obvious that he wasn't going to make any answer himself. 'He said you like him better than me because he's a boy.'

Regan clamped down hard on the reproof that sprang instinctively to her lips. If Jamie had indeed made that latter statement he needed putting straight, but taking Melanie's side against him right now wasn't going to help matters.

It took the puppy Melanie had already chosen as her own to sort out the situation, at least for the moment, by pouncing on her trailing shoelace with mini-growls. Laughing, she picked the little creature up again, holding it to her in an excess of love.

'I think you'd better have a word with him over this,' said Liam.

'I will,' Regan promised. 'When he's on his own. If he did say that he—'

'I'd doubt if Mel imagined it!'

'I don't suppose she did.' Regan maintained the steady tone. 'But something must have sparked it off. Jamie's the insecure one where you're concerned.'

'He doesn't need to be.'

'No?' She turned her head to meet his regard. 'Can you say in all honesty that you feel exactly the same for him as you do for Melanie?'

His expression hardened a little. 'That's an unfair question.'

'It's one we both need to consider.' Having got this far, Regan refused to allow herself any backing off. 'At least there's a blood tie between you and Jamie. I don't have any with Melanie.'

'Meaning you've no feelings for her at all?'

'That isn't what I said. She's a lovely little girl, and I'm sure we'll eventually forge a good relationship, but it's going to take time. The same with her and Jamie. They've got along well enough on the surface these last few weeks, but there's a big difference between the occasional meeting and actually living together as brother and sister. She's been used to having you all to herself, just as Jamie has with me. Learning to share on a full-time basis isn't going to be easy for either of them. There's bound to be some jealousy to start with.'

'Then we'd both better take care not to give one more attention than the other.' Liam sounded a little terse. 'Are we settled on these two, then?'

Regan accepted the change of subject without demur, aware of having nettled him. Yet all she'd said was the simple truth. There was no use blinding themselves to the difficulties that might lay ahead.

They called at a pet superstore on the way home to stock up on all the necessary paraphernalia. Reaching the house, the children could hardly wait for the car to come to a halt. The over-excited pups reacted predictably on emerging from their carry-cases into the alien environs of the kitchen. Regan cleaned up after them, only too glad that it hadn't happened in the car. It wouldn't be the sole accident for certain.

Hostilities recommenced almost immediately when the little animals failed to ally themselves to one child in particular, but showed the same, tail-wagging, tongue-licking enthusiasm whichever hand or face came within reach. Regan found it difficult to tell one puppy from the other without closer examination, though there was no doubt in either child's mind. It might have been a mistake getting two puppies, she reflected wryly. Given just the one, they would have been forced to share.

Liam settled things by threatening to take both animals back to the kennels if they didn't stop bickering. A temporary measure only, in Regan's view, but she could come up with no better solution.

She faced Jamie with Melanie's accusation the first chance she got, only to come up against a flat refusal to say what had caused him to make the remark. She tried not to make too much of the incident in the hope that it would soon be forgotten, thankful when the two of them started playing together again.

'A bit of masculine one-upmanship, that's all,' she told Liam. 'No great harm done.'

'Providing it doesn't get to be a regular thing,' he said.

'It won't, I'm sure.' Regan crossed her fingers as she said it. 'What do you fancy for lunch?'

The glint that lit the grey eyes signalled a lightening of mood. 'Guess!'

'Omelette?' she suggested, tongue-in-cheek, and saw the glint become a gleam. 'Not here,' she tagged on hastily as he made a move towards her, casting a glance across the room. 'The children...'

'I'm not suggesting going all the way,' he said with irony.

She made a rueful gesture. 'I just think we need to go a bit carefully, that's all. Let them get used to things gradually.'

'So what you're saying is it's hands off outside of the bedroom?'

'Something like that, I suppose. For the time being, at any rate.' She eyed him uncertainly, unable to judge his reaction. 'You do understand, don't you? It isn't that I don't want—'

'I understand perfectly,' he cut in. 'And you're probably right.' He moved again, this time towards the door, his composure absolute. 'I'll be sorting out the study. Give me a call when lunch is ready.'

Regan watched him out of the room, steeling herself against the urge to go after him, to shut the two of them in the study and prove just how much she wanted his attentions. She could hardly leave the children to look after themselves—to say nothing of the pups, who had already deposited a couple of puddles on the carpet. Most newly-weds just had themselves to think about; they had a ready-made young family. It was a totally different scenario.

CHAPTER EIGHT

JAMIE was due to start at his new school the same day his father returned to work, though with a great deal more reluctance. It wasn't fair, he complained, not for the first time, that Melanie should have all day to play with the pups while he had to do sums and such.

'Melanie will be starting school herself in September,' said Liam, beginning to sound more than a little intolerant. 'You've no choice in the matter, anyway, so settle your mind to it.'

'You'll have plenty of time to play when you get home,' Regan assured him, controlling the urge to sound off at Liam for his insensitivity. 'Not in front of the children' was the first rule in the book when it came to marital disputes.

'I think you were a little bit harsh with him,' she ventured when both children had left the breakfast table. 'Has it occurred to you that he might be feeling nervous about starting over with new people in unfamiliar surroundings?'

'He isn't a baby,' Liam replied firmly. 'So stop treating him like one. He has to learn that whining won't get him anywhere.'

Regan bristled at the slur on her son's character. 'That's unfair! He's six, not sixteen! If you had any understanding of children at all...'

Dark brows lifted sardonically. 'I don't think we're either of us in a position to claim expertise. Or are you claiming some special insight by virtue of being a woman?'

'I'm claiming to have a good grasp on what goes on in my son's mind!'

'*Our* son,' he said with point. 'Let's not forget that.'

'*Your* daughter,' she returned with equal thrust. 'Let's not forget that either!'

Regret was instant, the apology sincere. 'I didn't mean that the way it sounded.'

'I don't see which other way it could be meant,' he said. 'Perhaps it was expecting too much asking you to take on another woman's child, after all.'

'No!' She was eager to right the impression she had given. 'I want to get close to Mel. I want her to feel something for me—the same way I want Jamie to feel about you.'

'Which you doubt he will if I don't pamper him?'

Regan kept a tight rein on her tongue. 'I don't expect you to pamper him, any more than I intend pampering Melanie just to curry temporary favour. What we both need to do is make allowances.' She attempted to infuse a lighter note. 'Rome wasn't built in a day.'

'So I hear.' Liam glanced at his watch. 'I'd better be off. The traffic will be building already.'

'Wouldn't you be better going in on the train?' she asked, accepting the abandonment of what was, to her, a vital discussion with as good a grace as she could muster. 'I could always drive you to the station if you didn't want to leave the car there all day.'

He shook his head. 'Thanks, but, no, thanks. I'll take my chance on the roads.'

'What time can I expect you back?' she persisted as he got to his feet.

'Can't say for sure. If I'm going to be late I'll probably

eat in town. I'll give you a call this afternoon when I know what's what.'

'Right.' It was all she could say. The honeymoon—if it could ever really have been called that—was quite definitely over. 'I'll see you off,' she added in an attempt to keep at least some semblance of marital harmony going. 'Should I call the children?'

Humour briefly lit the grey eyes. 'All four of them?'

The pups didn't have to come too, Regan reflected, but refrained from voicing the thought. She went with him to the front door, lifting her face for a farewell kiss that left a whole lot to be desired. Perhaps she was the one expecting too much, she thought disconsolately, watching the tall, grey-suited figure descending the steps to the car already fetched from the garage.

The few days they had spent together as a family had been far from easy. There had been times when she had sensed a definite regret on Liam's part for ever having considered bringing the four of them together under the same roof. He'd still made love to her with the same ardour, but that was no more, she was sure, than he would do with any woman sharing his bed.

One thing he'd already made clear: he wanted no more children. Taking the problems they were experiencing with the present two into account, Regan could understand his feelings if she couldn't agree with them. She had missed so much of Jamie's babyhood. It would be wonderful to have the freedom to enjoy every minute of that time.

It was early days yet, anyway, she thought on the way back from the school where she had deposited a determinedly non-tearful Jamie. Once things had settled down, he might change his mind. Plenty of women had babies in their thirties, even in their forties. Her body clock had hardly started ticking as yet.

The intensive driving course Liam had booked for her had paid dividends in the shape of a first-time pass. The same day, he had presented her with the keys to the Mercedes 190 she was driving now. He'd given her so much. Far more than many men would have been inclined to do under the same circumstances. Materially, she wanted for nothing. Right now the housework was being taken care of by the super-efficient woman provided by the agency he'd contacted. She would have preferred someone a little less businesslike herself, but she wasn't the one doing to paying.

'I want Nana,' said Melanie suddenly from the rear.

'Perhaps we can go and see her this afternoon,' Regan responded on an upbeat note. 'Before we fetch Jamie from school.'

'I want Nana now!' came the prompt retort.

Start as you mean to go on, Regan told herself, hardening her heart. 'We can't go now,' she said. 'We have to take Cindy and Snowy for their walk. They'll be waiting. They can come in the car with us this afternoon.'

Torn between conflicting urges, Melanie was several moments coming to terms. 'I'm not holding Snowy's lead,' she announced at length.

'You don't have to,' Regan assured her. 'I'll look after Snowy. You just take care of Cindy.'

There was another pause. Regan glanced through the mirror at the pretty little face, wishing she could come up with something to put a smile there. 'Melanie likes everybody,' Liam had said at the start, and, once over the initial shock of meeting a brother she'd never even heard of, she'd certainly seemed to mellow towards him. That, however, had been before she realised just how much of an impact he was to make on her life. Regan doubted if at four years old she would have been any more amenable to being uprooted from the only home she had ever known to share her beloved daddy on an everyday basis.

They got back to the house to be met by an aggrieved Mrs Landers complaining that the dogs had made a mess on her freshly cleaned kitchen floor. Animals should be outside, was her outspoken opinion, to which Melanie responded with loudly expressed dissent.

Regan dealt with the situation as well as she was able by promising to shut the pups in the utility room when she wasn't going to be around to keep a watchful eye on them—a compromise that met with only limited approval from either side. What she should have done, she knew, was tell the woman that this was her house and *she* would decide what was or wasn't to be, but she couldn't summon the strength of mind.

The walk lifted both her own and Melanie's spirits. With two mischievous, full-of-vim-and-vigour pups to entertain, it was impossible not to join forces. Watching the little face light up, listening to her chuckles at the animal antics, Regan hoped this might spell the beginning of that breakthrough.

She spared more than one thought for Jamie, wondering how he was getting on. Starting a new school at any age was daunting; at six he could be forgiven for feeling totally overwhelmed. He was staying to school lunch because he always had, but it made it an awfully long day. It might have been better if she'd fetched him home for the first couple of weeks at least, she mused.

'Hallo again!' said a vaguely familiar voice, jerking her back to the here and now.

The man standing on the garden path a few yards away

registered her startled expression with some amusement. 'Sorry if I made you jump.'

'Uncle Dene!' Melanie came tearing across the grass, eyes sparkling with delight.

Laughing, he swung her up into a bear hug, planting a light kiss on one smooth cheek. 'Hallo, princess! Have you missed me?'

'Yes!' she cried.

He put her down again, flipping the pony tail she had insisted on having this morning, his smile teasing. 'About time you had this lot cut off!'

'I'm a girl, so I can have long hair,' she responded pertly. 'Boys are supposed to have short hair!'

He grinned, putting up a hand to flip his own blond pony-tail. 'Not this boy. It wouldn't fit my lifestyle.'

Which was what, exactly? Regan wondered. 'I didn't expect to see you again quite this soon,' she said.

'Had to see how things were turning out.' He bent again to greet the two pups as they came rushing up to inspect this new human, holding out a hand for them to sniff and lick. 'Liam certainly doesn't hang around when it comes to decision-making.'

'No.' She wasn't sure what to add to that. 'Let's put them back on their leads before they run off again,' she said to Melanie. 'They'll be ready for a sleep after all this exercise. How about coffee?' she added to Dene as her step-daughter complied without argument.

'Sounds good,' he said.

Melanie chatted without restraint to her uncle as they made their way back to the house. However Liam might feel about his adopted brother, it was obvious that he hadn't attempted to influence his daughter in the same direction. Regan could only respect him for that.

With Mrs Landers busy upstairs, they had the freedom

of the kitchen. Worn out, the pups fell asleep in a huddle in their basket, while Melanie herself started drooping. Dene carried her through to the smaller sitting room and laid her on a sofa, staying with her until she was fully asleep.

'Too much excitement,' he said, returning to the kitchen. 'She'll be right as rain after a nap, as Jean would say.'

'Jean?' Regan queried.

'I was a mite too old at twelve to start calling her Mom. Liam wouldn't have liked it, anyway.' The grin was appealing. 'We didn't get on from the start.'

Regan could imagine. The two of them were as different as chalk from cheese. 'Melanie obviously thinks the world of you, at any rate,' she said.

'Yeh. She's a great kid! I suppose I should be grateful Liam hasn't tried to turn her against me. Jamie seems a good kid too, from what little I saw of him when I was here last. I'd like to get to know him a bit better before I take off again.'

Why not? Regan asked herself. As she'd already told Liam, the feud between him and Dene was their business, not hers.

'I'll be fetching him from school at half past three,' she said. 'Why don't you stay to lunch and come along with us? Melanie would be happy to have you here for the day, I'm sure.'

There was no hesitation in the acceptance. 'I'd like that. You're real easy to be with.'

With Dene for company, the morning went by in a flash. He'd led a vastly entertaining life, with an endless fund of stories to tell. Melanie was delighted to find him still there when she woke up—especially when he fetched in the carved elephant he'd brought as a present for her.

'Indian,' he told Regan. 'I was in Delhi three days ago. Had to leave in a bit of a hurry.'

Regan refrained from asking why. She had a feeling she might not want to know.

Jamie emerged from school looking a great deal happier than when he'd gone in. There was a swimming pool, he said, with twice-weekly sessions for all pupils. He'd promised to take his certificate in to Show and Tell tomorrow.

He chatted happily to Dene, and vice versa, much to Melanie's disfavour. Dene not only teased her out of her sulk, but managed to draw both children into a game of improvised cricket back at the house.

'You're a natural-born mediator,' Regan told him, happy to see the two children in accord again. 'I wish I had the same gift. I'm finding it difficult to get through to Melanie.'

'She'll come round,' he assured her. 'Just keep plugging. You've done a great job with Jamie. He's a real little guy!'

'Mr Bentley on the telephone for you,' called Mrs Landers from the house before she could respond.

'His master's voice,' said Dene softly. 'Are you going to tell him I'm here?'

'Why on earth not?' she returned.

She took the call in the hall to save transferring possible grass stains from her shoes to the sitting room carpet. Liam sounded more than a little impatient.

'Where the devil were you?' he demanded. 'I've been hanging on for nearly five minutes!'

'I was outside playing cricket with the children,' she said levelly. 'How was *your* day?'

There was a brief pause, then he gave a laugh. 'Rough,

as you might have guessed. I wondered how you and Melanie got along on your own, that's all.'

'We weren't on our own,' she said, taking the plunge. 'Your brother's been with us most of the day.'

'Dene!' The humour had vanished. 'At whose invitation?'

'Mine, of course.' Regan allowed herself no backsliding. 'I know you're not enamoured, but Melanie obviously adores him.'

'Mel...' he began.

'I know. She likes everybody. Except me, that is.' Regan caught herself up, disgusted with the plaintive note she heard in her voice. 'Forget I said that. We'll get there eventually. When will you be back?'

'When you see me.' His tone was abrupt. 'I've an appointment at six. Tell Dene I'll speak to him tomorrow.'

He rang off before she could say anything more. Not that she had anything more to say. A lover's call it hadn't been.

'A hint not to be here when he does get home,' said Dene when she passed on the message.

'You don't have to go,' Regan told him firmly.

'Thanks, but it's time I was getting back, anyway. Jean said she'd have a meal ready at six.' He gave her a smile, eyes frankly approving what they saw. 'You're too good for him, you know. Given half a chance, he'll finish up walking all over you, the way he did with Andrea. There's no wonder she took off the way she did!'

Regan kept a tight rein on her emotions. 'There's no reason bad enough to excuse abandoning her own child!'

'Maybe she was unselfish enough to put Mel's needs first.'

'If that was the case, she'd have stuck it out regardless.'

Dene lifted his shoulders. 'Who knows? I'll say goodbyé to the kids. Okay if I come over again tomorrow?' he added casually. 'I've really enjoyed today.'

'Sure,' she said, refusing to allow the thought of Liam's reaction to put her off. 'I've enjoyed it too.'

She watched him cross the grass to where the two children were still displaying a fair degree of amicability while throwing balls for the pups. He was wrong, she was sure, about Andrea. The woman had left because she'd no desire to mother the child Liam had insisted she carry to term. Regan hadn't really known her all those years ago, but she had seen her a few times. From what she remembered of her, Andrea had been far from the type to allow herself to be walked over by any man. That had been *her* role back then.

Not these days, though. She'd learned her lesson the hard way. She owed Liam a lot, but she had no intention of letting him dictate who she did or didn't invite to their home. Dene was welcome any time he cared to come.

It was gone nine when Liam finally put in an appearance, the children long in bed.

'I had a lot to catch up on,' was his only explanation. 'I already ate.'

'So did I,' Regan answered, forbearing from adding that she'd waited until eight. 'Do you want a drink?'

'A whisky wouldn't go amiss.' He slung his jacket over the chair where he'd dumped his briefcase and came to take a seat on the sofa she had just vacated, easing back into the cushions with an air of relief. 'That journey twice a day is going to prove a pig!'

Building up to a suggestion that he use the apartment during the week already? thought Regan cynically, taking the whisky across to him like the good little housewife she was.

'It would perhaps be more convenient to stay in town

when you're working late,' she said with deliberation. 'Assuming that's why you kept the apartment on.'

Liam gave her a measured look. 'I kept it on,' he said, 'to use as a base when we're both in town for some function or other. Starting next week, as a matter of fact. We'll be entertaining a client and his wife.'

'We?' Regan was temporarily thrown. 'I don't—'

'Part of your wifely duties,' he said.

'Is it hell!' She was too angry over the presumption to choose her words. 'I married you for the children's sake, not to become a company asset!'

Dark brows lifted. 'I take it you'd have no objection to my finding a substitute, then?'

That pulled her up, but only for a moment. 'I'm sure you'd have no difficulty,' she said tersely.

Liam reached out a swift hand as she made to turn away, seizing her by the wrist to pull her none too gently down to the sofa beside him. He was angry himself, though in control of it, jaw taut. 'Is this attitude a sign Dene was here?' he said. 'I told you I didn't want him around!'

'I know what you told me,' she flashed. 'And *I* told you it isn't my affair!'

'Then you'd better make it your affair!' he snapped. 'I expect support from my wife.'

'Marriage doesn't mean giving up all claims to individuality,' she said with equal force. 'I'm entitled to keep an open mind.'

'Fine,' he returned. 'Just don't do it here.'

Regan drew in a furious breath. 'You're like a stuck record! And a boring one at that!'

'Be thankful we live in an enlightened age,' he advised, getting abruptly to his feet. 'I'm going to have a shower. Maybe an early night too.'

Blood boiling, she watched him stride from the room, his anger evidenced in every forceful movement. So typical of a man to walk away from an argument! Typical, and infuriating!

Rather more than just a mere argument, the part of her mind still capable of rationality suggested. A battle of wills in which Liam had come out the victor by very virtue of the fact that he *had* walked away. She felt suddenly and depressingly deflated. This was what came of marrying without love—on his part, at any rate.

And what about her part? asked that same rational little voice. If she really loved him, would she be contesting him the way she had these last minutes? She'd met Dene just twice; Liam had known him for much of his life. Of the two of them, who was best placed to judge character?

She went upstairs at ten, when it became obvious that he wouldn't be coming down again. Melanie had her elephant tucked into bed with her. Fearing she would catch her face on the upraised trunk if she turned, Regan gently extracted the carving, placing it at the end of the bed where it would be seen on waking. On impulse, she smoothed a tendril of dark hair away from the small forehead and bent to press a kiss. If not from the father, she could hope for eventual love from the daughter.

Jamie stirred when she tucked the cover back over him, but didn't waken. She lingered for several minutes, watching his sleeping figure—knowing she was just putting off the moment when she joined Liam in their bedroom.

Not that she needed to join him, of course. There were two other bedrooms to go to, one of them already made up by the super-efficient Mrs Landers in case of unexpected guests. It would do them both good, she decided, to spend some time apart.

Furnished and decorated to the same high standard as

the rest of the house, the room had its own *en suite* bathroom. It was only on undressing that she realised she had neither nightwear nor toiletries available. After these past few nights, the lack of the first was hardly a novelty, she reflected with irony, and she'd just have to manage without cleaning her teeth for once!

She was in bed with the lights out, though far from sleep, when the door opened. Framed against the landing light, wearing nothing but a towelling wrap, Liam looked as big and menacing as a grizzly bear.

'This,' he declared grimly, 'is *not* going to happen. Not in this family!'

Regan scrambled for the far side of the bed as he strode across, but she wasn't fast enough to evade him. Slinging back the sheet, he grabbed her round the waist to hoist her bodily out of it.

'Keep that up and you'll waken the children,' he said, stifling her protests. 'You're coming with me whether you like it or not!'

He carried her to their own bedroom like a sack of coal, dropping her on the four-poster bed with scant ceremony. Too furious to give a damn about her nudity, Regan levered herself upright, hair wildly tousled about her flushed face, eyes shooting flaming green arrows.

'So what's the next step?' she hissed. 'Going to claim your rights?'

'Rights?' Suddenly and astonishingly he was laughing. Not nastily, but in what looked and sounded like genuine amusement. 'You believe husbands have a right to sex on demand?'

Fury gave way to a growing mortification. 'You were giving every indication of believing it yourself,' she blustered in an effort to bolster her flagging spirit.

'I was giving every indication of a refusal to go along

with a gesture that benefits neither of us,' he said. 'A rather immature gesture, I might add.'

'So I'm childish now!'

'I didn't say childish. I said immature. Problems aren't solved by histrionics.'

Conscious now of her lack of covering, but reluctant to draw any further amusement by reaching for some, Regan forced herself to look him in the eye. 'They're not solved by ignoring them either. You were the one who walked out.'

'It was the only way to call a halt. Give us both chance to draw breath.' Hands thrust deep into the pockets of his robe, Liam regarded her in silence for a moment, a smile touching his lips as his gaze slid from her face down over smooth bare shoulders and creamy, jutting breasts. 'Not exactly a main priority right now, I have to admit.'

For her neither, Regan acknowledged, feeling the familiar tension in the pit of her stomach, the swift rising heat. She sank back onto the bed as he undid the belt of his robe with a flick of a lean brown finger and shrugged the whole garment from his shoulders.

He was so wonderfully built, she thought hungrily, feasting her eyes on the smooth muscularity of his upper body, the hard-packed midriff and flat masculine hipline. Standing over her, already fully aroused, he epitomised the dominant male, but in a sense that stirred her blood in a totally different fashion from the way she had felt downstairs. When he lowered himself to her she was ready for him instantly, wrapping limbs about him as they joined together, pressing feverish lips into the damp curls of hair on his chest, mind blanked of everything but the overpowering need.

She woke once in the night, to find herself still wrapped close in the masterful arms, his knees tucked up under hers. Like a pair of spoons, she thought mistily, loving the feel of his body moulded against her—loving the man himself despite their differences.

Those differences weren't going to go away, she knew. Liam expected too much in the way of compliance. All the same, was it really worth putting up a fight over Dene—especially when he'd probably be gone again in a couple of days? It was hardly as if he meant anything to her.

CHAPTER NINE

DENE failed to turn up the following morning. Warned off by Liam, Regan assumed, wondering just when contact had been made. While he might not mean all that much to her, she couldn't help regretting the loss of what had certainly been an entertaining companion.

Melanie missed her uncle too. She didn't see him often, she confided, but he always brought her lovely presents, and made her laugh. He must, she said, have gone away again.

Having first phoned to see if it was going to be convenient, Regan put both child and dogs in the car after lunch and drove over to Old Hay. They had called in twice the previous week, but there had so far been no attempt on either Jean or Peter's part to visit Copperlea.

The animals were no excuse, Regan considered. There were two kennel maids on daily duty. Which left her pondering as to the reason why. Understandable to a certain degree, perhaps, but hardly fair on Melanie, who had been accustomed to seeing her grandparents every day.

Jean greeted the child with delight, Regan herself with some reticence still.

'We thought you might prefer a little time on your own with Melanie,' she said when the latter's attention was occupied with the puppies' eager exploration of the unfamiliar kitchen. 'How are you getting along?'

'Slowly,' Regan admitted. 'The pups are helping. Where's Pal and Peg, by the way? They're usually the first to hear visitors arrive.'

'They're out in the runs. It was best with you bringing the pups over. They wouldn't harm them, but it would have been a bit much with all four of them prancing about. Nice little creatures,' she added judiciously. 'Excellent pedigree. Not quite house-trained yet, though, I see.' The last on the tolerant note only animal lovers could achieve as Cindy danced happily away from the puddle she had just deposited on the tiled floor.

'We're working on it,' Regan acknowledged wryly. 'Point me in the direction of a cloth and I'll clean it up.'

'We've known a lot worse,' Peter Bentley assured her. 'Don't worry about it. I'll do the cleaning up.'

'Did Uncle Dene go away again?' asked Melanie from her position flat on the floor wrestling with the two wriggling pups.

'Not yet,' her grandmother responded. 'He went to see some friends.'

'I understand he came over to Copperlea yesterday?' she added to Regan, lowering her voice a little. She made a rueful gesture. 'I asked him not to, but Dene always went his own way. I hope it didn't cause any trouble.'

'With Liam, you mean?' Regan kept her tone light. 'Nothing untoward.'

Jean hesitated, obviously wondering how much Regan knew. 'They've never been close. Dene was adopted, you see.'

'He told me.' Regan saw no point in holding back. 'What he didn't, Liam did. Apparently he's been a bit of a handful.'

'You could certainly say that.' Jean hesitated again, then gave a faint shake of her head as if in response to some thought. 'Liam did everything he could to keep him out of trouble—for what thanks he got. I'm afraid trouble and Dene were always interwoven!'

Even so, was it really enough on its own for Liam to turn so utterly and unyieldingly against the younger man? Regan mused. Could there perhaps be something more?

Dene hadn't returned when they left to go and collect Jamie from school. Arriving back at Copperlea to find him reclining on one of the terrace loungers was a surprise Regan could well have done without.

'I'm parked round the side,' he said in answer to her query, after greeting two delighted children. 'Just in case Liam decided to come home early. You know he's warned me off?'

'I gathered as much,' Regan said levelly. 'It doesn't seem to have made much of an impact.'

He grinned. 'I've a skin as thick as a rhino's! Especially when it comes to something I particularly object to being told. We got on like a house on fire yesterday. Why let a spot of jealousy spoil things?'

'Jealousy?' Regan couldn't help smiling. 'What does Liam have to be jealous about?'

'You and me, of course.' Dene was smiling too, a wicked sparkle in his eyes. 'I was always popular with the girls. It's the daredevil in me, I suppose. Not that I look on you as anything but a sister, naturally.'

'Naturally,' she echoed. 'As a bit of sisterly advice, I think you'd better be long gone before Liam does get home. He doesn't strike me as having much tolerance where you're concerned.'

The sparkle in no way diminished. 'Been hearing all about my exploits, have you? Dene the Deadly! One of the thoroughly bad lads!'

The children were far enough away not to overhear the conversation, if it could be called that. Mindful of last night's discord, yet reluctant still to be drawn into judgement purely on the strength of Liam's antipathy, Regan was torn by indecision.

'I'm not sure just how deep the trouble between you two goes,' she said at length, 'but I think it's probably best that I don't get involved. I'm sorry, Dene.'

He studied her in silence for a moment or two, an element almost of calculation in the hazel eyes. 'Are you going to let Liam dictate your whole life from now on?' he asked softly.

'Of course not,' she said. 'He wouldn't even try.'

'No? He seems to have you pretty much under his thumb already.'

'It isn't like that,' she denied. 'I simply think...'

'What he wants you to think. He's a control freak. Always was. If you let him, he'll do the same to you as he did to Andrea. You've no idea yet what an out-and-out louse he can be. She finished up hating his guts!'

Regan firmed her jaw. 'She told you that herself, did she?'

'Many times.'

'You were around more in those days, then?'

Some nameless expression flickered across the good-looking face. 'Off and on. I'd been on the receiving end myself, so I was the obvious one to confide in. Jean and Peter think the sun shines from him, of course. Their wonderful, brainy son!'

He caught himself up, conjuring his usual insouciant smile. 'Anyway, you can't say you haven't been warned.'

'I'll bear it in mind,' she said without particular inflection. 'In the meantime—'

'I know. It's better if I'm not here when he gets home.' He got to his feet, thrusting his hands into his jeans pockets as he regarded her. 'A real shame,' he murmured regretfully.

Regan watched him round the corner of the house, relieved to have him gone. It was all rubbish, what he'd said about Liam. A strong character he might have, but a control freak? At least it was unlikely that Dene would be paying any more calls, which obviated any further trouble. Unless the children mentioned it, she'd keep mum about this one too, she decided.

Apart from expressing a certain grievance over her uncle's failure to say goodbye, Melanie made little enough of it. She was well-accustomed to unexpected comings and goings on his part, Regan gathered. Of the two, Jamie was the more disappointed. Dene had been a temporary substitute for the father who was no longer available on a regular basis.

Liam was late again, this time not walking in until close on ten. Problems, he said, without going into detail. Sorted out now, hopefully for good.

'They'll see plenty of me at the weekend,' he declared when Regan mentioned the children's reluctance to go to bed without seeing him. 'We'll do something special.' He smothered a yawn. 'Right now, all I want is bed myself!'

'All?' she enquired with assumed ingenuousness, and drew a smile.

'Let's wait and see, shall we?'

He didn't let her down. In this sense, she had to be one of the best served women in the country, she reflected in the hazy aftermath of his lovemaking. Her period was due. That would give him a rest, she thought, smothering a laugh at the idea of his needing one.

'What's amusing you?' he asked, lifting his head to look at her.

'I'm just happy,' she said. 'Show me the woman who wouldn't be after being thoroughly ravished by a virtuoso!'

His grin was good to see, his regeneration even better to feel. Best *and* most regularly served, Regan appended as his lips claimed hers once more.

That was the good time. The bad time came three days later when she realised she was overdue.

The only time she'd ever been late before was when she'd got pregnant with Jamie, she recalled. It hardly seemed possible that lightning could have struck again. Liam was so against having another child. Two, he'd stated, were enough for any family. Perhaps if it had happened a year or so hence he might have been more amenable to the idea, but now he was going to go spare!

It wasn't absolutely certain yet, she assured herself, knowing, even as she thought it, that she was going to be bitterly disappointed if it turned out not to be. Another baby! The very notion made her yearn.

After two days of almost continuous rain, the weekend was fine and sunny. Liam's suggestion that they drive down to Brighton on the Saturday received enthusiastic support from both children, especially when told they could take the pups along too. Regan was on tenterhooks all the way, fearing 'accidents', but, with the benefit of regular stops, they arrived at their destination without mishap to spend a thoroughly enjoyable day all round.

'Great idea,' she said contentedly on the way home, with both children and dogs fast asleep in the back of the car. 'What do you have in mind for tomorrow?'

'A quiet day at home wouldn't go amiss,' Liam returned. 'I've barely seen the place this last week.'

'Sounds fine to me,' Regan agreed. 'Although I can't vouch for the quiet.'

'The price one pays.' There was a pause, a subtle change of tone. 'I'll be staying in town Monday night, of course.'

Regan sat up straighter, contentment flown. 'Monday night?'

'The dinner engagement I told you about. A VIP and his wife.'

She said slowly, 'You found someone to make up the party?'

'That's what you wanted, wasn't it?' His tone was dry. '"Not to become a company asset", I think you said.'

'I was…angry.'

He shrugged. 'Maybe with some reason. I was taking rather a lot for granted. Anyway, it's all taken care of.'

'So who did you ask?' Regan kept the question as light as she could.

'My PA offered to step in. She and the client's wife are around the same age, so they should get along okay.' Liam cast a sideways glance. 'No problems with that, I take it?'

'No.' She made a further effort to dissimulate. 'I couldn't have left the children in any case.'

'They'd have gone to Old Hay for the night. Dad would have been only too pleased to do the school run with Jamie.'

Immaterial now. He didn't have to say it. His PA would be no frump, for certain. Regan could just visualise her, sleek and sophisticated in a power suit calculated to emphasise a great deal more than just her business sense. There was every possibility that this wouldn't be the first time she and Liam had stepped out together—or perhaps even stayed in together.

She was building a whole scenario on nothing more than surmise, she told herself roughly at that point. If she hadn't been so bloody-minded about the dinner engagement in the first place there would have been no cause for suspicion. She had to start trusting him. With the chances of her being pregnant increasing by each non-productive day she had enough to worry about as it was.

The quiet Sunday at home proved anything but after Melanie suddenly asked if Uncle Dene would be coming to see them again soon. He hadn't even played with her the last time, she complained.

They'd eaten lunch out on the terrace. Liam waited until both children had finished and were away to play on the grass before letting rip.

'You had Dene here again after all I said?' he snapped.

'I didn't ask him to come,' Regan answered, keeping a tight rein on her own temper. 'He just turned up.'

'So why keep it a secret?'

'I didn't keep it a secret! I just saw no reason to mention it, that's all.'

'Placing rather a lot of reliance on the children staying mum, weren't you? Or did Mel forget instructions?'

Good resolutions went to the wall. 'I gave neither of them instructions to keep quiet!' she fired back. 'I didn't mention it because I knew exactly what your reaction would be. When you set against someone you don't let go! What actual proof do you have that he's up to no good these days?'

'None at all,' came the hard retort. 'What are *you* going on? Your feminine instincts?'

Green eyes flared. 'They're probably a darn sight more reliable than your biased ones! You've always resented him, haven't you? The adopted brother you'd far prefer never to have had!'

'Considering the trouble he's caused over the years, you're more than a little right.' Liam was speaking now with a restraint that carried more impact than his previous choler, a certain tension about his mouth the only sign of inner discord. 'Women always did find him attractive.

Maybe I was crediting you with rather more insight than you're capable of. Regardless, you stay away from him in future.'

Or else what? was the immature response that sprang to Regan's mind, though not, thankfully, to lips. She swallowed on the impulse, attempting instead to emulate his moderated tones. 'I'm not attracted to Dene. What I don't like is being told what to think about someone without adequate reason.'

Liam made an abrupt movement, shoving back his chair to rise from the table. 'Let's just leave it at that, shall we? I'm going to spend some time with the children.'

Regan voiced no protest. She wouldn't have known what to say. The division over Dene was only a small part of what ailed this marriage. Precious little trust from either side could be added to the score. Hardly the ideal atmosphere into which to bring yet another reliant being.

After placing what turned out to be a less than fail-safe reliance on Liam's precautions the first time, she should have gone on the pill, of course. She hadn't because deep down she had probably wanted this to happen, she reflected depressedly, wondering how and when she was going to tell him what she knew was almost certainly a fact.

The depression lifted regardless at the mere thought of what could be going on inside her at this very moment. Another baby: another small, helpless person to love and care for—and this time without outside help. Sarah had been so good with Jamie, but there was no substitute for a child's own mother. Liam would simply have to accept it, that was all. It might even draw them closer together in the end.

Watching him now as he threw a Frisbee for both children and dogs to race after, so lean and fit in the white shorts and T-shirt, she was suffused with mingled love and lust. Trust was supposed to be an intrinsic part of loving; she only wished she could attain it herself.

One thing Liam never did was allow discord to linger. When he finally abandoned the youngsters and came back to the terrace, he was smiling again.

'There comes a time when the flesh begins to tell on the spirit,' he declared, flopping down onto a lounger.

'You've just no stamina,' Regan scoffed, matching his mood. 'Comes of all that sitting around you do at work, I suppose.'

White teeth flashed as he grinned. 'If it weren't for certain little people, I'd show you how much stamina I have, lady!'

'Any excuse,' she mocked.

Looking at him, stretched out on the lounger, she gave way to sudden impulse and got up to go to him, dropping to her knees at his side to trace the firm lines of his mouth with a finger. 'I know we can't,' she murmured, 'but I want you!'

Liam put up a hand to cover hers, his eyes reflecting a mirror image of her own desire as he studied the captivating lines of her face within the frame of sunlight-reddened hair. He kissed her palm, sending a tremor coursing down her spine, said softly, 'The children are watching us.'

Regan refused to allow instinct any sway. 'It's time they realised that husbands and wives like a kiss and a cuddle themselves, now and then.'

'Like this?' he asked, and drew her down to him, holding her close while he suited his actions to her words.

'Exactly like that,' she said huskily when he let her face slide from between his hands again. 'Are they still looking?'

'Right now they're giggling.' Liam was amused himself. 'Seems we were worrying over nothing.'

'From what I recall, *I* was the one doing the worrying. And I still think it was right not to spring too much on them at once.'

The grey eyes crinkled at the corners. 'Whatever, it's a hell of a relief to be able to lay hands on you again.'

'As if,' she scorned in mock indignation, 'you've ever been deprived!'

'By night, maybe not. By day…you've no idea how hard it's been at times!'

Her laughter mingled with his. 'Nothing you couldn't cope with, I'm sure.'

Emotion swamped her as she gazed at him. The words trembled on her lips, held only by a lingering thread of self-preservation. Somewhere she had read that in every relationship there was always one member who loved more than the other. In *this* relationship there was no question of who carried the main load.

'Later,' he murmured, misreading the look in her eyes. 'I can just about wait.'

Expectancy low, the disappointment still cut deep. It was so obvious where his only real interest in her lay. 'You don't have any choice,' she said hardily.

She could feel his eyes on her as she pressed herself back to her feet, but she kept right on going. 'Things to do,' she flung over a shoulder.

She was stitching a button onto Jamie's school blazer when the five of them came indoors some time later.

'We're taking the pups for a walk now it's a bit cooler,' Liam said casually. 'Feel like coming along?'

Regan shook her head without looking up from her task. 'As I said, I've things to do.'

And all week to do it in, he could have pointed out. That he didn't said a lot for his forbearance, she admitted.

'I'm a bit tired,' she tagged on in an attempt to soften the refusal. 'Too much sun, maybe.' This time she did look up, unsurprised to see scepticism in the grey eyes. 'Don't walk them too far. They only have little legs.'

Liam made no answer to that. It wasn't, Regan was bound to acknowledge, the kind of remark that merited an answer. She was handling things all wrong, and she knew it; Liam wasn't the man to put up with swinging moods for long without seeking a reason. She could always blame it on hormones, of course. There was enough written about the havoc monthly cycles could sometimes create on a woman's disposition for men to have a little gleaning.

There was even a chance, came the fleeting thought, that her hormones really were beginning to play up.

She summoned a smile for the two children, thankful that they appeared to have mended their fences. 'I'll have your supper ready when you get back,' she said. 'Nice and early so it will be settled before you have your baths.' Oh, God, she thought, I sound like some old granny! 'Enjoy your walk,' she finished lamely.

'Enjoy your mending,' Liam responded drily.

Minus the children's excited chatter and the puppies' gambolling, the kitchen seemed almost too quiet. If she didn't take care, she was going to lose what feeling Liam did have for her, Regan told herself with force. He'd put so much into this marriage; the least she could do in return was satisfy his needs in what men considered the most vital department, without playing him up because he couldn't gratify her own most vital need. It was early days yet, anyway.

Not that her pregnancy, if it so turned out, was going to help at all.

True to her word, she had the children's supper ready by the time they returned. They were allowed to watch a Disney video afterwards. Liam joined them, laughing just as uproariously at the antics performed by the dozens of Dalmatian puppies.

'I shouldn't have thought that particular actress had it in her to lend herself to that kind of slapstick,' he said casually later when the children were in bed, the pups asleep in their basket, and they were eating the meal Regan had prepared while they had watched the film. 'Just goes to show how wrong impressions can be.'

Especially when too much was read into too little, Regan reflected. 'I was a boor earlier,' she said without preamble.

'Yes, you were,' Liam agreed. He rested a penetrative gaze on her face. 'Something I said?'

Something you didn't say, she could have told him. She lifted her shoulders, her smile wry. 'It's a female thing.'

'Ah!' The exclamation signified a certain resigned enlightenment. 'When are you due?'

If ever there was a time to tell him what she suspected, that time was surely now, Regan thought, but the words wouldn't come. 'Any time,' she said vaguely instead. 'Did you want dessert?'

Liam was oddly quiet for the rest of the evening, and for the first time made no move towards bedtime lovemaking, settling for a mere kiss.

'We both need to wind down,' he said.

Maybe he'd already had enough of her, thought Regan cheerlessly to herself as he turned away to thump his pillows into receptive shape. Helped along, no doubt, by her erratic temperament. Why couldn't she just accept things the way they were? Few people were fortunate enough to have it all.

Monday's weather was back to that of the previous week, with the added infliction of nigh-on gale-force winds. 'A typical British summer!' Liam observed, viewing the rain-swept scene from the shelter of the front doorway.

'I'll try and get back early tomorrow night,' he added. 'In the meantime, take care on the roads. It's not exactly ideal driving weather.'

'I don't have nearly as far to go as you,' Regan pointed out. 'And with a great deal less traffic to cope with.'

'I've driven for years, in all conditions. That's the difference.' For a brief moment, as he studied her, he seemed about to say something else, then the moment was gone. Eyes unrevealing again, he delivered the usual parting kiss, and left.

The day went through its phases. Deprived of outdoor activities, both Melanie and the pups got under Mrs Landers' feet, culminating in a scene which resulted in Regan suggesting that the woman find a job liable to better satisfy her exacting standards. She gave her a cheque representing three weeks wages in lieu of notice, and saw her off the premises with a real sense of relief to have sole command of her own home at last. If she needed help—and with a house the size of this one she had to admit that she probably would—then she'd look for someone herself. Meanwhile, she'd manage.

Her stepdaughter, for one, heartily approved the measure. Her stock, Regan gathered, had gone up by leaps and bounds. They spent the rest of the morning pastry-making, finishing up covered in flour but well-satisfied with the nineteen jam tarts they'd managed to salvage from the two-and-a-half dozen they'd started out with.

'What's Daddy going to say when he knows you've sent Mrs Landers away?' asked Melanie at lunch.

'He isn't going to say anything,' Regan replied firmly. 'If we didn't like her, that's all there is to it. Next time we'll find someone who knows how to smile!'

'And who likes puppies too!' said Melanie with a fond glance at the slumbering pair.

Jamie was entirely in agreement with his half-sister when he heard the news. He hadn't liked Mrs Landers one little bit, he confided. That made three of them, Regan reflected, wondering what the fourth member of the family was going to say about the summary dismissal. Not that it made any difference. *He* hadn't had to endure the woman.

She didn't bother cooking anything for her dinner, but made do with cold cuts from yesterday's roast, along with a salad. Perhaps foolishly, she had anticipated a phone call from Liam before he left the apartment, but by eight-thirty she knew it wasn't going to be forthcoming.

He would be with his client by now, she thought at nine, his PA at his side. It could have been her if she hadn't been so stupid. What had possessed her to come out with that ridiculous remark about company assets?

She went to bed at eleven-thirty, but found it impossible to sleep, her mind filled with visions of Liam and the woman he had taken to dinner in her stead. The meal would surely be over by now, the client and his wife departed. Liam would naturally feel obliged to take his partner for the evening home. The question was, *whose* home?

At one o'clock, unable to resist the urge any longer, she lifted the bedside phone and dialled the number, listening for several, increasingly heavy minutes to the unanswered trill. Either not there at all, or too occupied to even hear the call, she thought hollowly, replacing the receiver at length. Either way, it didn't look good.

CHAPTER TEN

TUESDAY seemed to last for ever. When Liam arrived, shortly after four-thirty, Regan was in the middle of cleaning up the mess the children and dogs had made on the kitchen floor, running in from the garden with muddy feet.

'I gave Mrs Landers the push,' she said, when he asked where the woman was. 'I'd rather do things myself than try to match up to her standards.'

Liam lifted a quizzical brow. 'She was working for you, not the other way round.'

Pushing back the damp hair from her forehead, Regan attempted a note of humour herself. 'Some people you just don't say that kind of thing to! Give me a minute to finish this, then I'll make some tea or coffee, if you prefer it.'

'If I was desperate for either, I'd make it myself,' he said. 'I don't expect to be waited on hand and foot. Where are the children now?'

'Upstairs in Jamie's room. All of them.'

'In disgrace?'

This time she had to laugh. 'Not so you'd notice. They're going to put some time into cleaning their shoes when they do come down. Two of them, at any rate. An eye for an eye is my motto.'

'Could run you into trouble at times.' Liam was smiling too. 'I have to admire your fortitude. Some women would be climbing the wall.'

His PA, for instance? Determined though she had been to keep such thoughts at bay, Regan found it impossible.

Suit jacket already shed, the sleeves of his pristine white shirt rolled to reveal muscular forearms, lean features relaxed, he was everything a woman could want in a man. His PA would be no exception for sure. And how many more?

'How did it go?' she heard herself asking.

'Last night?' He shrugged. 'Well enough. I'd have thought that floor was pretty well cleaned by now,' he added.

A definite avoidance of subject, opined Regan hollowly. Confirmation, if it was needed, that he had something to hide. Telling herself she was lucky to have what she had was no comfort.

Liam was going through the post he'd picked up from the hall table, tossing aside the obvious junk mail before slitting open the remaining envelopes with the edge of a kitchen knife to extract the contents.

'I'll be in the study,' he said after running his eyes down one particular missive. 'This calls for immediate attention.'

He made no attempt to say what 'this' might be about, and Regan certainly had no intention of asking. She finished mopping the floor, and put the cleaning materials away, catching a glimpse of her reflection in a nearby wall mirror as she closed the broom-cupboard door. Face shiny, hair all over the place, her yellow cotton shirt smeared down the front; she looked like something the cat had dragged in, she thought wryly. Hardly the kind of image scheduled to oust others from Liam's mind.

Children and pups were intermingled on the bedroom floor, along with several books and a couple of Melanie's soft-toy animals.

'We're showing Snowy and Cindy some pictures,'

Jamie announced when Regan popped her head round the door. 'They've never seen snow before!'

'Or cats,' Melanie chimed in. 'If we got a kitten too, they could all grow up together!'

'No kittens,' Regan declared firmly. 'No pups up here again either if they do anything they shouldn't. Daddy's in the study, and I'm going to have a shower, so stay where you are for the present.'

'Okay,' came the response in cheery unison.

Where they were concerned, the problems seemed to be over for now, thought Regan thankfully as she made her way back along the landing. There might be future spats, but hopefully only of the kind general between siblings. She could only trust that the baby, by now an accepted fact, wouldn't destroy the amity. Liam's reaction was going to be bad enough.

Showered, her hair washed and dried to a shining auburn cloud about her face, she steered clear on some inner urging of the trousers and shirt she'd been about to put on, choosing instead a long, swirly skirt in a silver-grey silk-Lycra mix, along with its matching, waist-length top. A touch of deeper grey eyeshadow, a sweep of the mascara brush and the application of a pale amber lipstick completed the transformation.

It was called fighting one's corner, Regan affirmed with new resolution. She had the weapons, so she'd use them!

Liam was still in the study when she went down. She made coffee and took it through, finding him seated at the desk with the computer switched on.

'Problems?' she asked when he failed to look up. 'Anything I can help with, maybe?'

'Not really,' he said. 'It's a—' He broke off as he finally lifted his gaze to where she stood, a smile curving his lips. 'Nice!' he said.

'An improvement on my previous appearance, at any rate,' she returned lightly.

'Oh, I don't know. I found *her* pretty appealing.' He got to his feet to come round the desk and draw her to him, the smile still lingering. 'You're beautiful in anything, green eyes! Out of anything too,' he added, ruining the moment with typical masculine prioritising. 'I missed you last night.'

When last night? was the thought that sprang to mind. 'I missed *you*,' she said, doing her best to forget last night. 'Especially after the night before. Were you angry about something?'

'Because I failed to perform?' Liam lifted his shoulders. 'After what you'd said earlier, I thought you needed breathing space. Most men find it difficult to know which way to jump when it comes to dealing with PMS.' He paused. 'I take it the pre is past?'

The moment of truth once more, Regan thought, but still couldn't bring herself to use it. 'Not yet,' she said instead. 'The stress is, though. I'm a veritable sea of tranquillity!'

'One I'll look forward to stirring up a storm in,' he promised. 'With a foretaste right now!'

Regan responded without hesitancy to the kiss, arms sliding about his neck, body moulding to him. If a fight was called for, then she was equal to it, she vowed. Whatever it took!

She spent an anticipatory evening. With the children in bed, she was more than once on the verge of suggesting an early night for the two of them too, but Liam seemed content enough lying back listening to a production of *Don Giovanni* on the radio. By ten o'clock, when the opera finally finished, she could hold out no longer.

'I think I'll go on up,' she said on as casual a note as she could manage. 'Are you going to be long?'

Liam gave a slow smile. 'And there I was thinking you'd never ask!'

'Of all the arrogant…!' Laughing, she launched herself at him where he lay supine on a sofa, kneeling astride him to pummel him with her fists. 'For two pins, I'd lock the door on you!'

Laughing himself, he grasped her wrists, holding her effortlessly. 'Not a chance!'

Regan collapsed onto him as he pulled her down, meeting his lips with a fervency undiminished from the last time. With his hands firm and possessive at her back, his masculine scent filling her nostrils, his body heat burning through her clothing, she was on the verge of forgetting everything else. It was Liam himself who called a halt, lifting her away from him with obvious reluctance.

'We'll continue this in a more secure venue,' he said. 'After I take the pups out for their last wander, that is.'

Regan got back to her feet, chagrined at her lack of circumspection. Between children and animals, he must feel really restricted, she thought depressedly as he went to see to the latter. She'd never been a career girl at heart, so she in no way missed her previous lifestyle, but Liam simply wasn't the type to take to domesticity wholesale. He belonged in the world of high finance, surrounded by those who spoke the same language.

She cut off that line of thought before it could reach its conclusion. He was *here* with *her* right now, and she was going to make the most of it.

Already in bed by the time he did come up, she lay watching with famished eyes as he undressed. Despite her vows, she found herself searching the smooth expanse of his back for tell-tale marks, such as might be made by fingernails, letting out her breath on a sigh when she found none. She could well be suspecting a great deal too much: the phone might even have been out of order last night, and not ringing at all at the other end. The very least she could do was give him the benefit of the doubt.

He came to her nude, his mouth a living flame in its passage from lips to breast to fluttering stomach muscle and soul-searing, body-arching intimacy. Lying in his arms after the tumultuous finale, Regan was filled with a whole new confidence. No man could make love the way Liam had just done, whisper the endearments he'd used, without feelings deeper than mere lust. So what if he hadn't actually said the three little words that meant so much to a woman? Many men were supposedly reticent when it came to expressing such emotions.

She could try setting the ball rolling by saying them herself, came the thought, but she couldn't summon quite enough will-power. If he said he loved her too she would never be a hundred per cent sure whether he really meant it or was merely reluctant to deny her. It had to come from him first. No matter how long it took.

'I can feel you thinking,' he murmured against her shoulder. 'You're vibrating with it!'

Regan gave a low laugh. 'I'm gathering myself for a counter-assault.'

'Sounds interesting.' Liam lifted his head to look at her, eyes glinting in the lamplight. 'What did you have in mind?'

She made no verbal answer, pressing him aside in order to sit up. Rolling onto his back, he watched her toss back the cover to its fullest extent, his regeneration already well under way.

She began at his feet, kissing each of his toes with butterfly strokes of her lips—working her way slowly and gradually up the full length of his body. By the time she reached his mouth he was almost at breaking point, turning her beneath him in one powerful surge to claim passionate possession.

'You're a woman of many parts, Regan Bentley!' he said eons later when he had breath to speak at all. 'And all of them sensational!'

A long way still from what she really wanted to hear from him, Regan acknowledged, but enough to be going on with. She'd intended taking the plunge and telling him about the baby tonight, only now it came to the point she hung back. Faint though it was, there was still a chance that it might be a false alarm. Why risk saying anything at all until she had absolute confirmation?

She received that confirmation the very next morning after driving into Weybridge to buy a pregnancy testing kit. There might be some slight doubt about a negative reading, she'd heard, but none at all with a positive. She was well and truly in the club!

It might help if she had someone to talk to, she thought ruefully. She considered ringing Sarah, but realised there was nothing her friend could tell her other than what she already knew. However little he might want it, Liam had to be given the news. And soon at that.

She called in at the village post office on the way to pick up Jamie that afternoon, in order to put a postcard in the window for a domestic help. Mrs Shentall, the postmistress, said she believed she knew the ideal candidate. She would tell the person in question to come up to Copperlea first thing tomorrow.

Regan hoped her idea of what constituted ideal was the same as her own. Another Mrs Landers she couldn't take. So far she hadn't suffered any of the symptoms she had experienced in the early days with Jamie, though they were no doubt going to come at some point. It would certainly be helpful to have someone around to look after Melanie at the times when nausea took over.

The phone call came around five. 'Mrs Bentley?' asked a cultured female voice. 'I'm Vivian Stevens. Your husband's PA,' she added when Regan failed to respond right away. 'He left a few minutes ago, but he forgot to give me some information I need to complete the job I'm working on. Could you ask him to give me a ring when he gets in, please? I'll be here until seven at least.'

'Yes, of course,' Regan said automatically, and, then, because she couldn't help it, 'How did the other night go?'

'The other night?' There was a pause. 'Oh, you mean the dinner engagement? It went very well. Such a shame you couldn't be there yourself, but it's understandable that you'd be reluctant to leave the children. It can't be easy taking on someone else's child—even as sweet a one as Melanie.'

'You've met her?' Regan asked slowly.

'Not exactly.' She gave a laugh. 'I suppose I'm seeing her through her father's eyes. It's taken such a load off him not having to worry any longer about her lacking the best kind of home life. He's very fortunate to have found someone happy to provide it.'

Which *she* certainly wouldn't have been, Regan inferred. 'Isn't he, though?' she agreed. 'Nice talking with you, Vivian.'

'You too,' came the reply. 'I'm looking forward to meeting you—and to seeing the house. It sounds idyllic!'

She rang off before Regan could ask the obvious question, leaving her to weigh the implications. They would be doing some entertaining once they were settled in, she recalled Liam saying, but surely not yet? She wasn't ready to meet a load of strangers. Especially not the one she believed might be a little more personally involved than her job called for. Vivian Stevens hadn't sounded quite the type she had had in mind, true, but the telephone was no conveyor of character.

She passed on the message as soon as Liam arrived, and left him to make the call while she went to supervise the children's bathtime. They'd become accustomed now to taking it together; Melanie had even gone so far as to discard her own floating ducks in favour of Jamie's fleet of boats. It said a lot for his emerging brotherly feelings that he allowed her to take part in his games.

Liam laughingly declined Melanie's invitation to join them in the bath when he looked in on his way to get changed.

'Big as it is, I think it might be just a mite crowded with three of us,' he said. To Regan he added, 'Vivian sends her apologies for pre-empting me. She was under the impression that you already knew about the party this weekend.'

'*This* weekend!' Regan couldn't contain her reaction. 'How on earth do you expect me to—?'

'I don't,' he cut in. 'I booked the caterers. It won't be a huge affair. No more than forty or so.'

'Oh, not many at all!' Regan cut off the rest of what she had been about to say, aware that the children were taking an interest. 'What's the occasion?' she managed on a calmer note.

'I believe it's known as a house-warming.' Liam sounded easy enough, but there was a certain tension about his jawline. 'I owe a whole lot of people hospitality. My mother offered to have the children and the pups overnight.'

Regan concentrated on refolding towels that didn't need refolding. 'So it's just for people *you* know.'

'Of course not.' His tone was still even. 'I contacted Hugh, and Sarah. They'll both be coming, along with their respective partners. It was meant to be a surprise for you.'

'The kind where I open the door in a dressing gown and face-pack to be greeted by a crowd all dressed to the nines, you mean?'

Liam slanted a sardonic eyebrow. 'Quite an image! I actually planned on telling you Saturday morning so you'd have all day to gild the lily. Not that you need it, but I never knew a woman yet who was happy with what Nature gave her.'

And he'd certainly known a fair number, came the fleeting thought. She made an effort to get things into perspective. So he'd taken it on himself to make all the arrangements for a house-warming party. Many women would be delighted not to have the hassle themselves. At least she would get to meet this Vivian—for what good it might do her.

'I guess there are worse ways of spending a Saturday evening,' she said, dredging up a smile. 'Worse men I could have married too.'

Liam returned the smile, albeit briefly. 'Possible. I'll see you two before you go to bed,' he tagged on for the children's benefit. 'Try not to swamp the whole floor!'

He carried on in the direction of their own room, leaving Regan to persuade the children out of the bath and into their nightwear. Liam was doing his best to adjust to domesticity, she chided herself. How many other men would have gone to the trouble he'd gone to over this party? Suspicions aside, she had a great deal to be thankful for.

She did her own best over the following few days to

concentrate on what was and stop worrying about what might be. The woman sent over by the postmistress turned out to be a widow in her late fifties who scored an instant success with Melanie by scooping up both prancing puppies in her ample arms with cries of delight. It took Regan bare minutes to decide that, with or without references, she was the ideal person for the job.

Jean Bentley's visit on the Friday came as a complete but welcome surprise.

'I thought it time I apologised for the way I reacted when Liam told us what was happening,' she said frankly when Melanie was otherwise engaged. 'I realise how wrong I was about you. I'm not usually given to snap judgements.'

'Understandable, I think, in the circumstances,' Regan assured her. 'I'd have been just as wary. Especially,' she tagged on with a smile, 'when Jamie doesn't even share Liam's colouring.'

'He has his bone structure, though,' replied the older woman. 'You can see it even now. Shares his temperament too. You'll need to watch that. Liam's level-headed enough on the whole, but he can be as hard as nails when he considers himself done down in any way.' She paused reflectively, then seemed to come to some decision. 'I don't suppose for a moment that he told you the real reason why he won't have Dene in the house?'

Regan looked back at her questioningly. 'The *real* reason?'

'He found out they were having an affair. Dene and Andrea. If the marriage hadn't already been rocky, it would have been a lot worse—especially with Melanie only a few weeks old. As it was, Andrea simply walked away from the whole situation. It turned out that Dene wasn't the only man she'd been seeing on the side.

Whether she's still with another man, I neither know nor care. Neither does Liam. He got full and permanent custody of Melanie. That was all he cared about. Naturally, he washed his hands of Dene.'

'I can see why,' Regan said softly. 'It must make things very awkward for you when he turns up.'

Jean gave a wry smile. 'Liam understands our position. When you adopt a child it's warts and all. Dene has his good points. He just got in with the wrong crowd at a vulnerable age. He was always a little jealous of Liam too, which didn't help. Anyway, you know now. I hope it helps *you* to understand.'

'It does,' Regan assured her. 'Very much so. And you're right; he probably never would have told me himself.'

'It's that damned male pride!' declared his mother. 'Anybody would think they were the only ones to have any! Lucky for them we women don't make the same hoo-ha over it.'

Some did, Regan reflected after her mother-in-law had gone. Wasn't it pride that kept her from letting Liam know how she really felt about him without being assured of his feelings first? Pride that stopped her from confronting him with her suspicions about Monday night. When it came right down to it, she was basing the whole thing on nothing more concrete than his supposed reputation as a womaniser still. It was time, she concluded, that she stopped chasing rainbows and grew up!

Saturday was fine and hot all day. People began arriving around eight. By nine o'clock the drive was lined both sides with cars.

'Forty, did you say?' Regan murmured to Liam as they went to welcome yet another party.

'I may have underestimated a bit,' he admitted. 'Lucky

I told the caterers around fifty. This lot would have my guts for garters if we ran out of food and drink!'

'"This lot" happens to include *my* friends too,' she said in mock indignation. 'Not that the numbers begin to compare, of course.'

'They will,' he promised. 'You look superb,' he added softly, running his eyes over the low-cut, body-skimming black dress as they waited at the door for the latest arrivals to slot their vehicle in among the others. 'I still find it hard to believe I could have let you go all those years ago.'

Regan swallowed on the sudden lump in her throat. 'It's all in the past,' she said. 'It's the here and now that matters.'

'Yes.' The grey eyes held an expression that made her heart beat suddenly faster. 'Regan, I—'

He broke off as the new arrivals came up the steps, donning a welcoming smile. 'I was beginning to think you'd got lost!'

'Accident just outside Richmond,' advised the silver-haired male half of the duo. 'Nothing too serious, but it took some time to clear. Lovely place you've got here!'

'Absolutely,' echoed the woman at his side. 'So much land to it too! All that grass is going to cost a fortune in maintenance!'

Liam laughed. 'I'll have you arrange me a loan.' He slid an arm about Regan's waist. 'Darling, I'd like you to meet Vivian and Richard Stevens. Vivian's my PA. You spoke on the phone the other day.'

Shaking hands, murmuring the appropriate responses, Regan was in a whirl. Well-dressed, and certainly attractive still, Vivian had to be in her early fifties. Even further from the image she had conjured in her mind's eye than the voice on the phone had indicated. Some men were drawn to older women, of course, but she doubted very much if Liam was one of them.

Not that it proved anything where other women were concerned. A leopard didn't change its spots.

With her mind on more important matters, she found it difficult to play the smiling, light-hearted hostess, her eyes constantly seeking the tall, lithe figure, so utterly devastating in the formal black and white. Physically she knew him through and through, but emotionally he was still to all intents and purposes a closed book. Perhaps he'd always remain that way.

The effort of making conversation with people who were mostly strangers eventually began to tell on her. What she needed was a few minutes' respite on her own, she decided, when one o'clock came and went with no sign of flagging on anyone else's part. The study seemed the likeliest place. No one was likely to venture in there. Just time enough to catch her breath, she promised herself, then back to the fray.

The room was in darkness, as anticipated. She didn't bother to switch on a light, sinking into the nearby chair and kicking off her high-heeled sandals with a sigh of relief. The window had been left open, she realised, feeling the draught of air on her face. She'd better remember to close it before she left.

It was more of a sixth sense than an actual noise that suggested another presence in the room. Sitting up straighter, her heart thudding, she said sharply, 'Who's there?'

The figure that rose from a crouching position behind the desk looked menacingly large against the lighter square of the uncurtained window. Regan dug her nails into the leather arms of her chair, wondering what on earth she could use as a weapon against what was indisputably an intruder. Her pent breath came out in an explosive sigh when the figure spoke.

'Don't panic. It's only me.'

Confusion took over from shock. 'Dene?'

'The same,' he acknowledged. 'Caught in the act, as you might say.'

'Doing what exactly?' she queried, trying not to let her thoughts get ahead of her.

He gave a short laugh. 'The sixty-four-thousand-dollar question!'

Regan got to her feet as he moved round from behind the desk, searching with her toes for her sandals. 'Put the desk lamp on, will you?' she said. 'I can't find my shoes.'

'Big problem,' Dene responded ironically, making no attempt to comply. 'I'd as soon stay in the dark, if you don't mind.'

With her eyes adjusting to the lack of light as she spoke, Regan found what she sought and slipped them back on, confidence rising along with the heel height. 'I'm still not sure what you're doing here,' she said. 'Unless you were thinking of gatecrashing the party.'

He laughed again. 'You reckon I'd be allowed to stay once Liam got wind of it?'

'He'd be unlikely to make a scene in front of everybody.'

'I wouldn't count on it. Not where I'm concerned.'

'Could you blame him?' she said with restraint. 'You slept with his wife.'

'It takes two,' he countered. 'And I wasn't the only affair she had.'

'*You* are his brother!'

'There's no blood tie.'

'You think that makes a difference?'

He shrugged. 'I can't say I've given it all that much thought.'

'You still didn't tell me why you're here,' she said, thrusting the rest aside.

'Simple. I'm in rather urgent need of money. I thought he might have some to hand.'

Regan was silent for a lengthy moment, hardly able to believe his effrontery. 'You mean you came to steal!'

'Desperation breeds desperation.' There wasn't the slightest tinge of self-reproach in his tone. 'He'd hardly be likely to listen to a direct appeal. Are you going to stop me?'

She controlled her initial instinct with difficulty. 'What do you need the money for?'

'Gambling debt. A rather large one.'

'Wouldn't Peter help if you asked?'

'Not unless he's changed his tune. Seems I might have to skip the country again for a while.' The pause was significant. 'Unless you could get round Liam for me.'

This time Regan made no attempt to withhold the boiling response. 'Get out of here!' she snapped. 'Just get out, you…parasite!'

Dene regarded her insolently, lip curling. 'Don't try playing the outraged innocent for me. We're not so different when it comes down to it.'

'You've got one minute before I call for help,' she said between her teeth. 'Assuming you came in through the window, you can leave that way!'

For a second or two he looked on the verge of defying her, then he lifted his shoulders, the sneer deepening. 'Sure. Can't have me ruining your game, can we?'

Regan waited until he was gone before moving to fasten the window, her limbs still shaky from the stress of the last few minutes. She was struggling with the catch when the door behind her opened without warning. The sudden flood of light as the wall switch was depressed held her in suspended animation.

'I've been looking for you,' said Liam. 'What on earth are you doing in the dark?'

'I remembered the window was still open from this morning,' she lied, ignoring the latter part of the question. 'I didn't want to leave it all night. You never know who might be around.'

'It would have been picked up by the alarm system when it was switched on.'

'Of course. I'd forgotten.' She attempted a smile. 'I'm just not used to these computerised gadgets.'

'You're not having much luck with that catch either. Probably needs adjusting.' Liam was moving as he spoke, coming across to where she stood to try locking it into position himself. 'Should be okay for now,' he said. 'I'll have another look at it in the morning.'

Turning away from the window, he paused as his foot caught something lying on the carpet. Regan drew in a ragged breath as he bent to pick up the black shoelace. Outmoded or not, Dene always used one to tie back his hair. It must have slipped off while he was climbing out through the window.

The expression on Liam's face when he looked at her left her in no doubt of his thoughts for once. His eyes were icy, his mouth a thin line.

'He's been here, hasn't he?' he clipped. 'You weren't just closing the window; you were letting him out!'

It was useless trying to deny it. Regan gave a helpless little shrug. 'All right, he was here. He's in trouble, Liam. He came to…ask you for help.'

'Via the window?' The sarcasm bit deep. 'Yes, I can

see that. Exciting is it? Having a man risk his neck just to have a few minutes with you in the dark!'

'It wasn't like that!' She was incensed by the accusation. 'I've told you before, I'm not in the least attracted to Dene!'

'I was fool enough to believe it too!'

Regan caught herself up before the too hasty rejoinder could leave her lips, moderating her tone. 'You can still, because it's true. I already told you why he came.'

'Oh, yes. He was looking for help.' His lip curled. 'If you're going to try lying your way out of this, at least make it plausible.'

'I'm not lying.' She said it between her teeth. 'Don't tar me with the same brush as Andrea!'

The grey eyes narrowed. 'What's that supposed to mean?'

'You know very well what it means. Your mother told me about her and Dene.'

'She had no damn right!'

'She thought *I* had a right to know why you were so against him. If you'd told me yourself I'd have shown him the door the very first time he came round.'

'Sure you would.' Liam obviously didn't believe a word of it. He added curtly, 'We'll continue this later. Right now we have guests to take care of.'

Regan bit her lip as he indicated she should precede him to the door. The very idea that she might have made some kind of assignation with Dene was ridiculous, if Liam would let himself see it. Only he wouldn't because he didn't trust her. Any more than she trusted him. They were each of them as bad as the other.

It was almost three o'clock when the last car departed.

'And a good time was had by all,' observed Liam cynically, closing the door as the tail-lights dwindled down the drive. The gaze he turned Regan's way was hard as iron. 'Still sticking to the same story, are we?'

'It's no story,' she said wearily, worn out from the strain of keeping up a façade these last couple of hours. 'Dene was after money, not me. I went to the study because I was feeling in need of a few minutes' respite.'

'Respite from what?'

'People—questions—innuendo.'

Dark brows drew together. 'Innuendo?'

'Jealous predecessors derive pleasure from sowing seeds. Not that they fell on unprepared ground. I've no illusions about this marriage of ours.'

'Meaning you believe I'll be indulging myself outside of it?'

Green eyes met grey full on. 'Isn't that what you're accusing me of?' She shook her head emphatically as he made to speak. 'Tonight wasn't proof of anything other than my stupidity in letting Dene get away with a criminal act simply because he's your brother. If you can't take my word for that—' She broke off, swallowing thickly. 'I'm going to bed. You please yourself.'

Liam caught up with her before she reached the stairs, his hands unexpectedly gentle as he turned her about. The coldness had gone from his eyes, replaced by an uncertainty she'd never seen in him before.

'We have to talk this through,' he said.

'What use is talking if we neither of us have any trust in one another?' Regan asked bitterly. 'If it hadn't been for the children you'd have no more contemplated marrying me than you did seven years ago. I've known that all along. I'm just a commodity!'

Anger flared again in the lean features. 'You're saying I've used you!'

'Well, haven't you?' She was past caring what she said,

wanting to hurt the way she was hurting. 'Oh, I've been well rewarded, I'll grant you. Some women might even consider it enough. Only not me. I'm greedy. I want it all!'

'And are you ready to give it all?' His voice was suddenly very quiet. 'Can you honestly say your feelings for me go any deeper than you believe mine do for you?'

'Yes!' she flung at him. 'They always did! I persuaded myself I could cope with it. I *was* coping with it until tonight. You've no idea what love really is, Liam. You never had!'

The reply was a long time coming, the grey eyes piercing her through. When he did speak it was gruffly. 'You'd have been right about that seven years ago, but not now.' He drew her to him, holding her close. 'You've no idea what I've gone through these past weeks thinking the children were *your* only incentive—having to more or less force you into marrying me at all! I could still stir you physically, but you gave no indication of anything deeper.'

'Neither did you,' she whispered, not yet wholly convinced.

The kiss went a long way towards it. She had never known such utter tenderness from him. She buried her face in his shoulder when he swept her up the way she had yearned for him to do on their wedding night, loving his strength, his purpose. There were things still to be said, but they could wait. This was enough for now.

They made love like two people starved of contact for years. Lying replete in his arms in the dawn light, Regan drifted on a tide of pure happiness, no doubts left. Liam loved her: he'd proved it in every way this past hour.

'I wasted seven years,' he murmured against her hair. 'Seven years when we could have had all this!' He drew back a little to look at her, devouring her face feature by feature as if to imprint it on his retinas. 'Seeing you coming across the room that night was like being transported back in time—given another chance. I was totally thrown when you gave me the cold shoulder. Even more so on hearing you were supposedly involved with a married man old enough to be your father. I wanted to punish you for not being the girl I remembered, only once I'd touched you I just couldn't leave it at that.'

Regan brought up both hands to cup the lean face, tracing the line of his mouth with her thumbs. 'Neither could I. I've tried to convince myself that I never meant to blurt it out about Jamie, but it isn't really true. I wanted you to come after me.'

'I'd have done it anyway, once I'd cooled down and accepted that meeting you again and knowing there was still something there between us was the important thing,' he said. 'I was even more determined after getting the truth from Hugh. There was just no way I was going to let you slip through my fingers again. Jamie came as a shock, I admit. It was hell realising how much of his life I'd missed.'

'I'm sorry,' Regan said softly.

'My fault, not yours. All of it was my fault.' He shook his head. 'How the devil you can love me after—'

She stopped his mouth the best way she knew, putting heart and soul into the lingering kiss. 'I never stopped loving you!' she declared huskily when they surfaced at last. 'You ruined me for other men!'

'*All* other men?' he queried after a moment.

'*All*,' she confirmed. 'I couldn't bring myself to even think about making love with someone else.'

Liam looked as if he didn't know quite what to say for a second or two. When he did speak it was with a certain diffidence. 'I realise I've no right, but I'm not going to pretend to be anything but glad about that.' He paused again, jaw constricting. 'I must have been insane giving you up for Andrea!'

'She gave you Melanie,' Regan reminded him. 'So it wasn't all bad.'

'That part, no.' There was a pause, a change of tone. 'You said Dene was after money?'

Dene was the last subject she wanted to discuss, but it couldn't be avoided. 'Yes. He said he'd run up a huge gambling debt, and might have to think about leaving the country if he couldn't come up with the money.'

'The kind of people he plays around with, it would be a wise move.' Liam paused, adding resignedly, 'I'll settle it this time, but he's on his own after that.'

'It's more than he deserves,' she said.

His expression softened as he looked at her. 'You're more than *I* deserve, green eyes. You always were. One thing I can promise you, there won't be any playing away on my side. I've got everything a man could possibly want right here.'

Rather more than he knew as yet, she thought wryly.

'I did harbour certain suspicions regarding your relationship with Vivian Stevens,' she said, still shying away from telling him about the baby.

Sudden amusement creased his face. 'Vivian!'

'Well, I didn't know until tonight how old she is. I couldn't imagine you having a PA old enough to be your mother.'

'Only just. And I choose my staff on the basis of ability not age. Vivian's been my right hand for the last five years. I hope she'll be with me for at least another five. What made you suspect her anyway?'

'She was the one you asked to go with you to meet that client and his wife.'

'Only because you wouldn't come with me. It did work out better, as it happens. The wife wasn't the type to welcome an evening in company with a much younger woman—especially not one looking like you.' He eyed her quizzically. 'Is that it?'

'I phoned the apartment around one. There was no answer.'

'Hardly surprising. We were with the Gordons until gone half past twelve. By the time I'd put Vivian in a taxi and made it to the apartment it was going on for two. Checking "caller display" was the last thing on my mind at that hour.'

'You must think I'm an idiot,' Regan said ruefully.

'It's going to take time to convince you that I've abandoned past habits,' he returned without rancour. 'But I'll keep working at it.'

'You've put in a lot of effort already,' she murmured. 'It can't be easy for you being landed with all this.'

'Landed?' Liam both looked and sounded disconcerted. 'Is that how you really believe I feel?'

Green eyes searched grey uncertainly. 'Well, don't you? You've been used to living your own life at your own pace. In the week, at any rate. Now you're faced with a whole family. You must find it all pretty daunting at times.'

He lifted himself on an elbow, smoothing back the tendrils of hair from her face with a tender hand. 'One thing we need to get clear. I've no regrets whatsoever about losing my so-called freedom. Sure, it took a bit of adjustment at first. It must have done for you too. But there hasn't been a solitary moment when I've wished things were back the way they were. We *are* a family. And we're going to stay a family. All four of us!'

'Six,' Regan corrected. 'You're forgetting the pups.' She sobered again, recognising that the moment could be put off no longer. 'Seven in a few months' time, in fact.'

Liam showed little surprise. 'I was beginning to suspect as much.'

'You don't mind?' she asked.

'It's a bit late for minding, although I might consider suing a certain manufacturer for supplying shoddy goods.' He smiled at the look on her face. 'Only joking. I'd have preferred a little more time to enjoy what we already have, but what the hell! The more the merrier!'

'How about trying for the round dozen?' Regan suggested tongue-in-cheek, laughing at the look on *his* face. 'Only joking.'

'You'd better be,' he growled. 'Any more slip-ups, and I'll start to suspect sabotage!'

Green eyes widened innocently. 'As if I'd even think of it!'

He chuckled in response, eyes kindling once more as he gazed at her. 'It's daylight. I suppose we should get some sleep.'

'Later,' she said softly, drawing him down to her again. 'Right now it's the last thing I need.'

HARLEQUIN *Presents*

Passion™

Looking for stories that **sizzle**?

Wanting a read that has a little extra **spice**?

Harlequin Presents® is thrilled to bring you
romances that turn up the **heat**!

Every other month there'll be a
PRESENTS PASSION™
book by one of your favorite authors.

Don't miss
THE ARABIAN MISTRESS
by **Lynne Graham**
On-sale June 2001, Harlequin Presents® #2182

and look out for
THE HOT-BLOODED GROOM
by **Emma Darcy**
On-sale August 2001, Harlequin Presents® #2195

Pick up a **PRESENTS PASSION**™ novel—
where **seduction** is guaranteed!

Available wherever Harlequin books are sold.

HARLEQUIN®
Makes any time special ®

USA Today bestselling author

STELLA CAMERON

and popular American Romance author

MURIEL JENSEN

come together in a special
Harlequin 2-in-1 collection.

Look for

Shadows and *Daddy in Demand*

On sale June 2001

HARLEQUIN®
Makes any time special ®

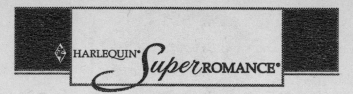

HARLEQUIN *Super*ROMANCE®

To celebrate the
1000th Superromance book
We're presenting you with 3 books
from 3 of your favorite authors in

All Summer Long

Home, Hearth and Haley
by **Muriel Jensen**
Meet the men and women of Muriel's
upcoming **Men of Maple Hill** trilogy

Daddy's Girl
by **Judith Arnold**
Another **Daddy School** story!

Temperature Rising
by **Bobby Hutchinson**
Life and love at St. Joe's Hospital are as feverish
as ever in this **Emergency!** story

On sale July 2001
Available wherever Harlequin books are sold.

HARLEQUIN®
Makes any time special ®

Harlequin truly does make any time special.... This year we are celebrating weddings in style!

A Walk Down the Aisle
WEDDING CELEBRATION

To help us celebrate, we want you to tell us how wearing the Harlequin wedding gown will make your wedding day special. As the grand prize, Harlequin will offer one lucky bride the chance to **"Walk Down the Aisle"** in the Harlequin wedding gown!

There's more...

For her honeymoon, she and her groom will spend five nights at the **Hyatt Regency Maui.** As part of this five-night honeymoon at the hotel renowned for its romantic attractions, the couple will enjoy a candlelit dinner for two in Swan Court, a sunset sail on the hotel's catamaran, and duet spa treatments.

A HYATT RESORT AND SPA

Maui • Molokai • Lanai

To enter, please write, in, 250 words or less, how wearing the Harlequin wedding gown will make your wedding day special. The entry will be judged based on its emotionally compelling nature, its originality and creativity, and its sincerity. This contest is open to Canadian and U.S. residents only and to those who are 18 years of age and older. There is no purchase necessary to enter. Void where prohibited. See further contest rules attached. Please send your entry to:

Walk Down the Aisle Contest

In Canada	In U.S.A.
P.O. Box 637	P.O. Box 9076
Fort Erie, Ontario	3010 Walden Ave.
L2A 5X3	Buffalo, NY 14269-9076

You can also enter by visiting www.eHarlequin.com
Win the Harlequin wedding gown and the vacation of a lifetime!
The deadline for entries is October 1, 2001.

HARLEQUIN®
Makes any time special ®

PHWDACONT1

1. To enter, follow directions published in the offer to which you are responding. Contest begins April 2, 2001, and ends on October 1, 2001. Method of entry may vary. Mailed entries must be postmarked by October 1, 2001, and received by October 8, 2001.

2. Contest entry may be, at times, presented via the Internet, but will be restricted solely to residents of certain georgraphic areas that are disclosed on the Web site. To enter via the Internet, if permissible, access the Harlequin Web site (www.eHarlequin.com) and follow the directions displayed online. Online entries must be received by 11:59 p.m. E.S.T. on October 1, 2001.

   In lieu of submitting an entry online, enter by mail by hand-printing (or typing) on an 8½" x 11" plain piece of paper, your name, address (including zip code), Contest number/name and in 250 words or fewer, why winning a Harlequin wedding dress would make your wedding day special. Mail via first-class mail to: Harlequin Walk Down the Aisle Contest 1197, (in the U.S.) P.O. Box 9076, 3010 Walden Avenue, Buffalo, NY 14269-9076, (in Canada) P.O. Box 637, Fort Erie, Ontario L2A 5X3, Canada.

   Limit one entry per person, household address and e-mail address. Online and/or mailed entries received from persons residing in geographic areas in which Internet entry is not permissible will be disqualified.

3. Contests will be judged by a panel of members of the Harlequin editorial, marketing and public relations staff based on the following criteria:

   • Originality and Creativity—50%
   • Emotionally Compelling—25%
   • Sincerity—25%

   In the event of a tie, duplicate prizes will be awarded. Decisions of the judges are final.

4. All entries become the property of Torstar Corp. and will not be returned. No responsibility is assumed for lost, late, illegible, incomplete, inaccurate, nondelivered or misdirected mail or misdirected e-mail, for technical, hardware or software failures of any kind, lost or unavailable network connections, or failed, incomplete, garbled or delayed computer transmission or any human error which may occur in the receipt or processing of the entries in this Contest.

5. Contest open only to residents of the U.S. (except Puerto Rico) and Canada, who are 18 years of age or older, and is void wherever prohibited by law; all applicable laws and regulations apply. Any litigation within the Provice of Quebec respecting the conduct or organization of a publicity contest may be submitted to the Régie des alcools, des courses et des jeux for a ruling. Any litigation respecting the awarding of a prize may be submitted to the Régie des alcools, des courses et des jeux only for the purpose of helping the parties reach a settlement. Employees and immediate family members of Torstar Corp. and D. L. Blair, Inc., their affiliates, subsidiaries and all other agencies, entities and persons connected with the use, marketing or conduct of this Contest are not eligible to enter. Taxes on prizes are the sole responsibility of winners. Acceptance of any prize offered constitutes permission to use winner's name, photograph or other likeness for the purposes of advertising, trade and promotion on behalf of Torstar Corp., its affiliates and subsidiaries without further compensation to the winner, unless prohibited by law.

6. Winners will be determined no later than November 15, 2001, and will be notified by mail. Winners will be required to sign and return an Affidavit of Eligibility form within 15 days after winner notification. Noncompliance within that time period may result in disqualification and an alternative winner may be selected. Winners of trip must execute a Release of Liability prior to ticketing and must possess required travel documents (e.g. passport, photo ID) where applicable. Trip must be completed by November 2002. No substitution of prize permitted by winner. Torstar Corp. and D. L. Blair, Inc., their parents, affiliates, and subsidiaries are not responsible for errors in printing or electronic presentation of Contest, entries and/or game pieces. In the event of printing or other errors which may result in unintended prize values or duplication of prizes, all affected game pieces or entries shall be null and void. If for any reason the Internet portion of the Contest is not capable of running as planned, including infection by computer virus, bugs, tampering, unauthorized intervention, fraud, technical failures, or any other causes beyond the control of Torstar Corp. which corrupt or affect the administration, secrecy, fairness, integrity or proper conduct of the Contest, Torstar Corp. reserves the right, at its sole discretion, to disqualify any individual who tampers with the entry process and to cancel, terminate, modify or suspend the Contest or the Internet portion thereof. In the event of a dispute regarding an online entry, the entry will be deemed submitted by the authorized holder of the e-mail account submitted at the time of entry. Authorized account holder is defined as the natural person who is assigned to an e-mail address by an Internet access provider, online service provider or other organization that is responsible for arranging e-mail address for the domain associated with the submitted e-mail address. **Purchase or acceptance of a product offer does not improve your chances of winning.**

7. Prizes: (1) Grand Prize—A Harlequin wedding dress (approximate retail value: $3,500) and a 5-night/6-day honeymoon trip to Maui, HI, including round-trip air transportation provided by Maui Visitors Bureau from Los Angeles International Airport (winner is responsible for transportation to and from Los Angeles International Airport) and a Harlequin Romance Package, including hotel accomodations (double occupancy) at the Hyatt Regency Maui Resort and Spa, dinner for (2) two at Swan Court, a sunset sail on Kiele V and a spa treatment for the winner (approximate retail value: $4,000); (5) Five runner-up prizes of a $1000 gift certificate to selected retail outlets to be determined by Sponsor (retail value $1000 ea.). Prizes consist of only those items listed as part of the prize. Limit one prize per person. All prizes are valued in U.S. currency.

8. For a list of winners (available after December 17, 2001) send a self-addressed, stamped envelope to: Harlequin Walk Down the Aisle Contest 1197 Winners, P.O. Box 4200 Blair, NE 68009-4200 or you may access the www.eHarlequin.com Web site through January 15, 2002.

Contest sponsored by Torstar Corp., P.O. Box 9042, Buffalo, NY 14269-9042, U.S.A.

PHWDACONT2